THE
MAGDALENE
GATES

THE MAGDALENE GATES

A *Novella*

Richard G. Geldard

Larson Publications
Burdett, New York

ISBN-10: 1-936012-90-1
ISBN-13: 978-1-936012-90-9
eISBN: 978-1-936012-91-6

Library of Congress Control Number: 2019938870

Publisher's Cataloging-In-Publication Data
(Prepared by The Donohue Group, Inc.)
Names: Geldard, Richard G., 1935- author.
Title: The Magdalene gates : a novella / Richard G. Geldard.
Description: Burdett, New York : Larson Publications, [2019]
Identifiers: ISBN 9781936012909 | ISBN 1936012901 | ISBN 9781936012916 (ebook)
Subjects: LCSH: Mary Magdalene, Saint--Correspondence--Fiction. | Jesus Christ--Teachings--Fiction. | Letters--Fiction. | Man-woman relationships--Greece--Fiction. | Spirituality--Fiction. | LCGFT: Romance fiction. | Thrillers (Fiction) | Novellas.
Classification: LCC PS3557.E374 M34 2019 (print) | LCC PS3557.E374 (ebook) | DDC 813/.54--dc23

Published by Larson Publications
4936 NYS Route 414
Burdett, New York 14818 USA
https://www.larsonpublications.com

28 27 26 25 24 23 22 21 20 19
10 9 8 7 6 5 4 3 2 1

GATE NUMBER ONE

THE DRAWER is stuck. Tonio crouches down to get a better look at the faded label in its dented brass holder. He laughs.

Jean-Marc looks up from his computer. "Qu'est-ce?"

"I thought it said, 'Safe House.' You know, where the FBI hides people . . . or something."

"Ah. And?"

"It must be 'South East Fountain House' in some shorthand from the mid-Fifties. OK. Once more." He stands and stretches his back. Jean-Marc nods and goes back to his keyboard. Above Tonio's head, the fan turns slowly, barely moving the warm, damp air through the long storeroom with its rows of glassed-in shelves and stacks of drawers. Tonio wipes the sweat from his hands on his shorts and prepares to try the drawer again.

Jean-Marc pauses to watch, and as Tonio crouches down again, Jean-Marc intones, "And now, mesdames et messieurs, Tonio Fletcher, American graduate student, bon vivant, very temporary fellow of the American School of Classical Studies in Athens, seeker of mysteries, slave of the ancient Agora, is poised on the edge of a great discovery and will attempt for you . . ."

"All right! Hush, I have to concentrate here." Tonio had been slumped over his workbench for two hours, since just after nine, and with the heat, the lousy light, and the dust, he felt seventy-five instead of twenty-five. He bends over again and gets as good a grip on the small wooden knobs as he can and pulls. The left side gives way with a pop. A smell of mold escapes, and he sneezes.

"Dieu vous benisse!" Jean-Marc says solemnly, crossing himself in mocking reverence.

"Merci, mon père." Tonio hits the drawer with the heel of his palm. It goes back in. He tries again. This time it opens straight, revealing, for the first time in probably fifty years or so, an assortment of pot shards, marble fragments, pieces of terra cotta water pipe, and odd pieces of Roman tile gathered over a century of work in Athens' ancient marketplace. He sneezes again as he picks out a piece of shard, turns it over to see if he can read the notation. What crap. It slips from his damp fingers and falls on a piece of terra cotta. The piece breaks. "Damn," he breathes. He closes the drawer partway and wipes his hands on the red-checked bandana he keeps by his stool. Eyes closed, he waits until the blood stops pounding in his ears. He picks up a paper bag with his lunch in it. "I'm getting out of here," he announces

Jean-Marc looks over at him. "Lunch already?"

Tonio looks at his watch. Eleven-twenty. "No point in coming back for only a few minutes. I need air, such as it is. See ya." Jean-Marc says nothing.

Tonio passes through the outer office and quietly slips past Daniel Marrins, his other colleague, who is on the phone with his back to Tonio. He is making little clucking noises. Daniel has a new friend, evidently.

Out on the wide, glaring white porch of the stoa, Tonio side-steps a group of tourists and bounds down the stairs. On the Sacred Way he walks quickly through a blast of hot air and sun up to the abandoned north gate and out of the Agora. Jean-Marc and Daniel will be angry with him, of course, for leaving thirty minutes before lunch break. But hell, he has good cause to be really pissed about being stuck in that storeroom, for being in Athens at all—snatched in from the field, from his real work, by Field Marshall Director Robert Templeton of the American School, who has set him down in this junkyard and told him to label the trash. Being stuck in the Agora storeroom in July is like being stuck in summer school when all the other kids are at the beach. And he's never failed anything. Never has.

He turns left along the eastern wall of the Acropolis and finds his spot along the fence, the one between two overgrown Rose of Sharon shrubs, where he won't be seen climbing over. Putting a bare arm up to protect his face from snapping branches, he pushes in through to the six-foot, wire-mesh barrier. He grips his lunch bag in his teeth and climbs up and over, avoiding, this time, catching his shorts on the sharp steel barbs along the top and not very artfully, truth be told, drops to the slope on the other side.

He loses his balance on the incline and tries to right himself but falls back against the fence post. The blow knocks his breath out and he drops his lunch. He kneels on the dry grass for a moment, sucking in air. Little squiggles of light dance before his eyes. Nice play, Tonio.

Seeing this rather pitiful exercise, Daniel would shake his head in disbelief. Darling, he said last week, accept that fate has landed you here in prison and be gracious. One summer, that's all, and your nights are your own. Sure. Tonio sits up, picks up his lunch and himself, and continues up the slope. When he comes to the narrow path that hugs the great Acropolis wall, he emerges into the sun again and continues more slowly around to the precinct of Dionysus and the ancient theater. His back twinges with every step.

It is true, he must admit, that all this effort in the heat of an Athenian July is stupid, or as Jean-Marc would intone, "Stooo-peed!" The fence trick, he knows, is just his way of saying up yours to Dr. Templeton, who would no doubt make his life very difficult if he were caught sneaking into the theater site. Tourists, of course, have to pay a separate admission to get in here and, as a result, seldom enter the famed Precinct of Dionysus. He, on the other hand, being beyond all that, is damned if he will pay admission just to sit and eat his lunch in peace.

He sits down lotus-like in a small piece of shade against the wall of the Acropolis, eating a falafel and lettuce pita and takes sips of lukewarm coffee saved from the morning's work. Below, the Theater of Dionysus, once home to Oedipus, Agamemnon, and even the god Dionysus himself, sits unused, a derelict. To lovers of everything Greek, the perfect circle once sacred to Classical drama had been chopped in half by the Romans for their circus entertainments. So mutilated is its former beauty that the space is seldom visited, unlike the perfection of the Theater at Epidaurus, where plays are mounted all summer and into fall.

Between bites he sits quietly, eyes closed, listening to the hum of idling tourist buses lining the road outside the gate, when he hears the chatter of voices of a group entering the precinct. It is a group of twenty or so boys and girls, high school age, he thinks, in the company of two adults and a guide. One of the adults, a teacher no doubt, is wearing an actual pith helmet. He sits down on a column drum and fiddles with his cell phone.

The guide, a woman, enters the theater orchestra and stops exactly where the ancient altar would have marked the center. She is thin, boyish almost, dressed in sandals, khaki shorts, an oversized white tee not tucked in, and a white cap with a blue visor. She raises an arm and with a languid gesture motions the group to gather around her. As she begins to speak and point to places in the space, the ethereal waving effect seems as if her arms have no bones. It is a beautiful motion, mesmerizing. Tonio stops breathing, stops chewing. A piece of lettuce hangs from his mouth.

The students follow the guide's gestures with slow movements of their own as they are being directed. She is literally conducting the group as if rehearsing a tragic chorus. She turns and looks up the slope, seemingly right at Tonio, although he can't be sure. He can hear very little above the humming buses. At Epidaurus, in the quiet and perfection of that space, he would hear every word, even at the back of the theater.

Tonio glances at his watch. Still time. He will go down. Circle around to the side. He has to see this person up close. Without taking his eyes off her, Tonio puts his wrap down on its paper, pockets his journal, and begins working his way slowly down the slope toward the orchestra. As he gets closer, he can see that the light cotton cap is pulled down low on her forehead, and round sunglasses glint in the sun when she turns her head. Edges of shining black hair show around the cap and wisps cling to her neck in the afternoon heat. Her skin is deeply tanned, her nose straight and thin, and the curve of her chin is gentle and rounded up to small ears, softening the effect. He moves closer.

She is discussing tragedy. Her accent is French, but there is something clipped and formal in the inflection. Tonio sits down on a stone seat near the west parados. This close, he can read the blue inscription on the white polo shirts many of the kids are wearing. It says Hellenic Studies Program under a Greek flag insignia.

"I want you to imagine this space as it was," she is saying, "when the great playwrights were producing plays here. Forget this Roman destruction, if you can. The orchestra was a large dirt circle, like the threshing circles we saw last week in the hills near Bassae. The seats were wooden, plain, no fancy marble seats for so-called 'important' people as you see there. It was a theater of ideas and feelings, not spectacle. Can you imagine this?"

Students nod. Cell phones raised, a few snap pictures. She goes on. "You can see the top of the Parthenon from here. It would have been more visible then than it is now. The sun came up over the hills behind the theater striking the temple first. No trees, no fences, no apartment buildings. Just language and precise movement. The sounds of the double flute in the silence. Story, passion, sun, fate, and death. All mixed together, nothing separate. Very intense, like sun coming to a point through a magnifying glass. Burning into the mind."

When she stops speaking, Tonio breathes again. For a moment he is light-headed, and he puts a hand to his forehead to shield his eyes. One of the girls asks a question about Antigone, something about being led away to die in the cave. She calls the guide My-ah. It must be Maya or perhaps Maia, the Greek name. Perhaps she is Greek. She looks Greek. Exotic anyway.

She turns to listen to the question and then lifts her arm toward the great Acropolis wall. "Find the iron gate at the base of the wall," she says. "In the fifth century there would have been a deeper cave there. It was the place Antigone was taken to be buried alive. The audience imagined her taken there, where she hanged herself and where her lover Haemon died, too. These are human matters, tied to time and place, and not just empty myths. Sophocles wanted us to feel this death, to know it well and yet to survive it and to feel the rising sun on our faces. You see this? Yes?"

Several students nod. She turns away from the orchestra and moves away from where Tonio is sitting. One boy sits in the High Priest's marble chair while someone takes pictures.

Someone calls out, "One more, Kevin. Like that, yah." "Aw'right." High fives.

"Come this way now," the guide calls. "I want you to see the work on the Pericles Odeion, not the ugly Roman Odeon of Atticus back there, but the Greek one. Pericles celebrated Greek victories over the Persians by building the Odeon. It was modeled after the great tent of Xerxes."

As the group moves away, Tonio pulls out his journal and makes a note:

Deep cave in Acropolis wall? Antigone's tomb? Guide in theater said so. How can she know that? Dramatic focus in theater like sun through a magnifying glass! Great image that. What threshing circles near Bassae? What is she talking about? Roman frosting on stale Greek cake. Ha! Next time you go to Bassae, look for threshing circles.

The group climbs up through the seats and gathers around the guide as she points to remnants of retaining walls and the work in progress. Again, her gestures seem to evoke some silent chorus and bring the site to life.

Tonio is drawn to follow but doesn't. As he climbs back up to the Acropolis wall, he watches the guide as she conducts the group. He can't hear her now, but it doesn't matter. Her arms float up into the afternoon heat and lift him up the slope. He must find out who she is. But how? There were hundreds of groups like this one busing around Athens. He could have asked down there when the kids looked over at him. Could have said, Hey, where are you guys from? But she was speaking, and he couldn't. Maybe the logo on the shirts will help. He glances at his watch and sees that he is late, again. He picks up his half-eaten lunch and hurries around the corner of the site and down the path.

At the stoa, Tonio walks across the wide marble porch and stops in the office to get coffee and finish his wrap. He sits down at the Director's desk. Daniel Marrins looks up from his screen. "Ah, Tonio, my boy, returned at last from whatever land to the safety of friends and family."

"I have been missed, I gather?"

"Of course. We are a little club, a tiny fish-bowl. So where do you go, if I may intrude on your carefully preserved privacy?"

"Around to the southern slope. I have this theory about there being an Aphrodite temple . . ."

Daniel laughs. "Come on, Tonio. That's no theory. It's just old news. There's nothing there and you know it."

"No, I don't know it," he said, standing. He goes over to the coffee pot.

Daniel stops typing and looks at Tonio seriously for a moment. "Don't snip at me, dearest. If you find even one foundation stone over there, what with all the afflatus clogging up that site, I'll kiss . . . well, I can dream can't I?" He looks away.

Tonio stirs sugar into his cup. The mood clears slowly. "Sorry Daniel. It's hot out there."

Daniel throws up his arms. "Then for God's sake, stay inside and be a good boy. But come up with better stories, at least." His freckled face is red. He types.

Tonio smiles. "OK. Fine. Tell me, how would you find a group touring sites in Athens. Do they register or what?"

Daniel stops, looks at Tonio. "Indeed, let's change the subject. Does this group have a Greek guide?"

"I think so, yes. I'm not changing the subject actually."

"Then," Daniel continues, "the guide will be registered with the Greek Cultural Office, where they also keep tabs on all groups moving around this ruin-wracked, ghastly country. I imagine they would have a record of what guides are doing what and where."

"Know anybody there? A name I could use?" Tonio asks.

Daniel spreads his hand over his chest, feigning shock. "Moi? Certainly not. You could call Judith, however. She's in touch with the natives one way or another in her site work. She will no doubt be in the Institute library this afternoon. Give her a ring." Daniel turns to his computer, then looks up again. "But somewhere in the day, rummage through a few drawers, will you? I am starving for data. Starving!"

Tonio smiles. "I will, Daniel. Don't worry." He finishes his coffee and goes to the door of the museum office. He pauses and turns to Daniel, who still looks bent out of shape, his lips pursed. "Hey, listen to this: the dramatic action in the Greek theater was like the sun focused through a magnifying glass upon a burning point. What do you think?"

"Very nice. Did you just come up with that?"

"No, I heard it . . . from a guide."

"My goodness," Daniel says, smiling now. "I must get out more." They laugh. Tonio goes into the alcove and dials the main school number and asks for the library. Judith Diels would be at her special table, surrounded by her papers and index cards, her white hair pulled back into a neat Germanic bun. Judith is an archaeological legend in Athens, she who knows the location of every cult site and ruin within the city limits, who dedicates herself to cataloguing every single one to protect the antiquities from the crush of downtown development.

Her voice comes on the line. "Diels here."

"Judith? Tonio Fletcher."

"Ah, Tonio. I was thinking of you the other day, about your work. How is it going?"

"Stuck as I am here in the storerooms, I'm not doing much in the field. Much, hell, nothing."

"What happened? It's this terrible transition business, yes?"

"That's it. Dr. Templeton pulled me in from Mycenae just as I was getting started on tomb measurements and said that I was needed, desperately needed as he put it, to complete cataloging before the Greeks take over. So here I am."

"And not happy about it, I surmise."

"To put it mildly." Tonio says. "It looks like a wasted summer, in more ways than one."

"I understand. Do you have any help?"

"They called in Jean-Marc Lucard from the French Institute, and of course, Daniel is here doing all the data entering."

"That's something," Judith says.

"Look, Judith, I'm calling because I need to locate a group touring around. They're here in Athens now and they have a Greek guide, at least I think she's Greek. Daniel thought you could help."

"Ah, let's see," Judith replies. "If the guide is Greek, you can call Nikos Skouros at the Cultural Office and get a name as long as you can identify the group. Do you know where they are from?"

"It's an American high school group. Can't be too many of those around. I suppose I can piece enough together. Thanks much."

"By the way, Tonio, I like your overall thesis, you know. I'd like to talk to you about it before you go back."

"Sure, I'd like that."

"Have you been to Samos?"

"No. I've never gotten out there. Why?"

"Development dates from the Bronze age and there's Mycenaean evidence, probably as early as 1200, and it has some landscape features you might find productive.

"Thanks, I'll call you later," he says. "You know, Judith, it's been so long since anyone has offered encouragement on this project, I hardly know how to react."

"Stick to your guns, my boy. Stick to your guns."

"I wish I had a gun to stick to. I might use it." Judith laughs. "Anyway, thanks again, Judith. I'll talk to you later. I have to make this call and get back to my precious shards."

Judith says, "Call me when you want to talk," and hangs up.

The next morning in the storage room, Tonio is sitting alongside Jean-Marc as they methodically catalogue. The tired overhead fan sways and rattles as it moves the warm air through the room. A steady ping, ping, ping marks the passing moments. The only other sound is the rasping of Daniel's printer in the other room. Tonio picks through the drawer of shards from a draw marked "Fountain House," each marked with a date and site number. These are all odd pieces, none fitting together. It's like doing a hopeless jigsaw puzzle, one with no pictures, no clear shape, and mostly missing pieces. A sharp pain moves from his neck down his back to his side. He tries shifting his position. Finally, he works standing up.

A little after eleven o'clock, Daniel relieves the tedium.

"Tonio, Templeton is on the phone, wants a word."

"Oh, mon Dieu, mon Dieu," moans Jean-Marc. "His Immenseness has called for confession. May peace and peace . . ." He signs a cross in the air.

"Don't get started," Tonio snaps, as he makes a note on his sheet and carefully replaces a shard in the drawer.

He calls out to Daniel. "Is he holding?"

Daniel leans back into the room and in a loud whisper, "Yes, but by all means take your time. He sounds quite matter-of-fact, even asked me if I was enjoying my work." He rolls his eyes.

Another look at Jean-Marc draws a shrug as Tonio leaves the room. Dr. Templeton seldom calls or comes to the stoa. He isn't 'one of the gang,' preferring, it seems to Tonio, the role of authority and maker or breaker of careers. A lover of hierarchies. Tonio notes the knot in his stomach as he steps into Daniel's office. He won't be surprised if Templeton asks what he was doing in the theater, spies being everywhere.

Tonio picks up Daniel's phone. "Fletcher here." He mimics Judith Diels.

"Tonio, Templeton. I need a favor. A group from my old school is coming to the Agora this afternoon, and usually I give them the tour, but I have to be at a meeting to smooth our little transition. I thought perhaps you could walk them around. They're stopping at Eleusis on their way up to Delphi later in the afternoon, so they won't have long. Show them the Eleusinian along with the usual. You know. They're coming to the South gate after an early lunch, I would guess around one-thirty. Can you do that for me?"

Tonio's mind is racing. It is her group, has to be. Would she come with them? Sometimes the Greek guides stay away out of deference to the Americans. But why wouldn't she come?

"Tonio? Are you there?" Templeton asks.

"Oh, yes, sir, uh . . . that's fine, I was just calculating . . . how long do I have? I mean, should I take them around to the rest of the Agora, or into the museum?"

"Their faculty fellow tells me the bus will be at the gate no later than three for the trip north, so I suppose a quick glimpse of the storage rooms if you want. Tell them something about what you all are doing. There may be a future archaeologist in the bunch. Got to go. Thanks for helping out, should be fun. They're a bright group. Good school. Oh, and tell the faculty people I'm sorry to have missed them."

"Yes, sir, I'll meet them, and thanks for thinking of me."

"Let me know how it goes," Templeton adds, "I shall have to write a letter to the school and make my apologies." Templeton hangs up.

When Tonio puts down the phone, Daniel looks up from the computer. "Some group coming in?"

"American preppies. Templeton's old school, in fact. He says he's off to a transition meeting. What's that about?"

Daniel shrugs. "Just the usual dickering about money, I'll wager."

Tonio leaves the office with a wave of his hand, looks at his watch, and heads back to work.

As he sits down at his bench, Jean-Marc glances over. "Still among us? Not packing up?"

"Au contraire, mon ami," Tonio says. "À vrai dire, I am Dr. Templeton's personal emissary to the Agora this afternoon and will be conducting a tour of the site in his stead. Thus, while you, poor soul, continue to perish in butt-numbing oblivion, I shall be sharing my brilliant insights with the privileged youth of America." Jean-Marc sweeps his hand through the air in mock tribute.

The work is slow and oppressive as the room collects the afternoon heat. Tonio's head is filled with ways to start a conversation if indeed the guide does come. Ask about Antigone. The cave in the great wall. What is that reference? Where does it appear? In the play? Would there be time for that? How would he give a tour and still have time to speak to her? If he brings them here, Jean-Marc can explain their work. He will find a way of speaking to her.

A little after one, they stop for a break, venture outside, and find shade. Daniel joins them.

Jean-Marc leans against the wall. "Drosia," he murmurs, almost to himself.

"What?" Daniel asks.

Jean-Marc looks up. "Drosia," he repeats, letting the word roll out into the warm air. "It's a word the Greeks have for escaping from the heat, finding a cool, dew-laden place at high altitude. I think it has a . . . ana . . . poetic . . . what is that word in English?"

"Ono-mato-poeia," Tonio enunciates.

"Yes, that's it," Jean-Marc says. "I intend someday to find a large piece of drosia somewhere in the world and settle there."

Daniel laughs. "Hanging out in Greek storerooms won't get you there."

Jean-Marc is silent for a moment. He shrugs. "Yes, well, c'est ça." He turns to Tonio. "So, Hermes, how will you guide these awe-struck children? Will you praise archaeological research, the virtues of the dig and the diggers, find the new Schliemann in their greedy American minds?"

"You are speaking here," Tonio says, "to the son of two teachers, brought up in a household devoted twenty-four hours a day to meticulous preparation and unfaltering responsibility. I don't think I could vary from that narrow line of heredity even if I felt the urge. Anyway, these are nice kids."

"How would you know?" asks Daniel.

Tonio pauses. "I mean, they must be very bright, coming from a good school, cream of the American crop, that sort of thing. Templeton's old school. He extolled their virtues to me when he called." He smiles. Tonio looks at his watch and stands. He turns to Jean-Marc. "I'm going to bring them by the storeroom. Templeton's idea. Maybe you could explain what we're doing?" Jean-Marc squints up at him. He wrinkles his nose.

"You know, research, meticulous cataloguing?"

Jean-Marc snorts "I will pretend I know no English. Perhaps I will be your mentally defective servant. They will think you keep me as a pet."

Tonio turns to Daniel. "Work on him, please." He walks toward the South gate.

There, where a small hut serves to sell tickets, maps, and guidebooks, Tonio plants himself in an old folding chair under a plane tree and watches the crowds milling around the shops across the narrow street. Faded Olympic 2004 tee-shirts, music from Zorba the Greek from an equally faded cassette player, all as it has been now for years.

GATE NUMBER TWO

THE GUARD at the gate reads the morning paper, holding it down as swirls of dust spin up from the path in tight little circles. Traffic across the submerged rail line rattles along the cobblestones. Mopeds and motorcycles weave sputtering among the pedestrians as workers hurry home for lunch and the long afternoon siesta. They will roar back after four o'clock for another few hours of work and then turn around and do it again for a second time. It makes no sense but the old ways die hard, even with Athens converting finally to more of a ten-to-ten tourist economy. After all, the tourists never rest and they need constant service. The Greeks endure long summers of resentment, serving as waiters to a hungry EU culture.

A flurry of white shirts catches Tonio's eye as the group of boys and girls dash across the main street. He looks for the guide, but she isn't among them. The group assembles in a knot around the gate. One of the teachers, the pith helmet, a sheaf of papers in his hand, follows when the light turns and negotiates the group fee at the booth. Tonio walks over and introduces himself, apologizing for Templeton's absence.

"No problem," the teacher says, helmet in hand, wiping his forehead. He leans close to Tonio, bowing slightly from the waist.

"Frankly, the kids will enjoy someone more their own age anyway. This is fine." He turns to the group. "Everyone? This is Dr. Fletcher. He'll be guiding us through the Agora this afternoon. So, stick close and pay attention." He turns to Tonio. "Lead on, Macduff."

As Tonio drops back, he turns to the students walking along with him and explains that he isn't yet a doctor of anything and to call him Tonio. He glances toward the gate and sees her—still across the street, waiting for traffic. Tonio stops. After waiting for the light, she crosses over and approaches the group. She pulls her sunglasses down over her eyes and slips a small white package into a cotton sling bag draped over her shoulder. She looks directly at Tonio for a moment and then gives her attention to three boys who crowd around her and with boyish admiration seem to mimic her graceful movements as they describe their morning. She smiles briefly and with mock gravity waves them ahead.

As they walk along, Tonio explains the site. He takes them first up to the Temple of Hephaestus, where, just below the temple, a large diorama of the Agora marks the essential ruins. The guide stays in the rear, watching Tonio and the students. Occasionally she speaks to stragglers. Tonio takes them next down to where the American School found the ancient State prison where Socrates might have died. He shows them the pit where a dozen small vials were found, refuse from doses of hemlock. Maybe even the one given to Socrates. The guide seems interested and moves closer and looks for some time at the foundation stones of the prison site. She lingers for a few moments when the group moves on.

Following Tonio over to the stoa, the class gratefully gathers in the shade of the long, marble porch. He explains the modern restoration and points out several of the better sculpture fragments on display. He takes a moment and talks about archaeology in general and about his own field work, the examination of tholos tombs in ancient Mycenaean sites throughout Greece.

I understand," he says, "that you have been to Bassae, in the Peloponnese. The precinct of Apollo you saw there was also sacred to his twin sister Artemis. The ravines, the glens, the springs in Elis suggest the forms of the goddess. The temple seems to sit on the reclining body of the goddess. In fact, the earliest temple there was probably dedicated to Artemis, back in the seventh century. But perhaps your guide has already explained this to you." He glances over at her. She smiles but says nothing.

Walking the group back to the Stoa, Tonio turns to the side door of the museum. He guides the group through the office, introducing Daniel, and then into the storeroom, where Jean-Marc sits contemplating a broken bust of Athena. The group stands still, waiting. Jean Marc sighs heavily and looks up, languidly. Tonio introduces him.

Jean-Marc begins speaking in French and then feigns horror at their lack of understanding. He shifts to a stumbling English at least three degrees below his ability and begins to explain the work taking place. "Er, ze scholar which undertakes ze work here must have ze incrimination, yes?" The students laugh. Jean-Marc shrugs and stumbles on. "Here we have ze piece of pot. Lovely, no?" Tonio is relieved.

He moves over near the guide, who had remained by the door to Daniel's office. "Is there anything you would like to add, uh, while we're here? I, uh, don't know what to call you."

She looks at him, removes her sunglasses and, for the first time, smiles. A beautiful, very brief smile. Her eyes are dark, almost black. Tonio sees himself in their depths. She looks him over very frankly. "Maia Spiros." Before he can speak, she adds, "What you said about the tholos tombs. Is that your work? And you were in the theater yesterday as well, am I right? Is this too an area of interest?"

Tonio reddens. "Yes, the tholoi are my work. I . . . uh . . . was also interested in what you were saying . . . said there about Antigone. I came down because so very few groups come into the precinct. Sad really. I wondered who you all are, which is why I came down."

"As you said." She smiles again. "What about Antigone interested you?" She seems to choose her words carefully.

"You said that she was confined to a cave above the theater, up where I was sitting, actually. I had never heard that. That grotto is still active. I mean visited sometimes by women with offerings."

"Yes, it is sacred to women who are near death or who know death as a companion." She glances at her watch. "The bus is waiting. But to answer your question. In the Antigone, I believe it to be just after line one thousand, where the actor playing Creon must actually point out a place above the theater and says, 'in that place overlooking us.' In the Greek it is *epopsion topon*. You can find it, I'm sure. And now we must go. Thank you for your time. I know how busy you are. The students were quite good, don't you think?" She turns to leave.

Tonio says hurriedly, "Yes, very good . . . wait, please . . ." Students press behind him as he stands in the door. "I wonder if . . . when you return to Athens, if we might discuss this further. It's very interesting."

She steps to one side, Tonio following, as the students pour out of the stuffy room onto the stoa porch. She waits for them all to pass before she turns. The teacher pauses to speak to Daniel. Maia watches the group and then turns to Tonio. "I am not going on to Delphi. I must leave the group today." She looks after the group as it moves through the stoa, then turns back to Tonio. "I am, however, most interested in your work. Is it possible that we might, perhaps this evening, have dinner?"

"Yes, of course. What interests you about tombs, in particular, I mean?"

Maia smiles again. "Perhaps at dinner. Can we meet at ten o'clock, in the Plaka, at the corner of Adrianou and Kleous? Do you know it?"

"Adrianou and Kleous, yes, I think so."

She smiles again and turning, leaves, trailing the group. Tonio follows along with the bobbing pith helmet, listening to it talk about how clever Dr. Spiros is and how much the group has learned from her, how much they will miss her now, but she is unwell, evidently, he says, and how much he loathes long bus rides, but at least the road to Delphi is mostly highway. They stop at the gate.

Tonio watches Dr. Spiros as she crosses the street. Unwell? He hears one student call "Maia?" and run to catch up with her. Tonio says good-bye to the teacher, shakes his hand, and watches the group move toward a sleek blue-and-white tour bus waiting at the curb. The door opens with a hiss. Students pile in. A few stay behind and say good-bye to Dr. Spiros. She kisses one or two and then shooes them onto the bus. As it leaves the curb and merges slowly into traffic, she waves, that slow fluid movement of her right arm that Tonio thought later was a wistful gesture. Then she turns and walks quickly down to the avenue. Tonio thinks about following her but doesn't dare. She disappears in the crowd.

At ten o'clock the Plaka is still alive with tourists. All the stores in the narrow streets are brightly lit, some blaring bousuki music. Old men with black caps sit on folding chairs and watch the women as they pause to look at jewelry or fondle cotton dresses. Tonio reaches the corner and finds a wall to sit on. Maia Spiros arrives just after ten. She's wearing a pale blue dress, and her hair is different. She smiles. They stand together for a moment on the street, Tonio not sure how to begin.

"Thank you for coming," Maia opens. "Would you let me select a place to eat?"

"Certainly," Tonio says, surprised at his formality, as if she were a nun or something. He's deferring to her. Is she a contemporary? Or an 'older woman?' He's listening for signals and, as he had that afternoon, speaking as he is spoken to.

"This way," she says and turns down Diogenous Street until they come to a garden restaurant tucked into a corner, where the road curves. A dozen tables are arranged under a huge plane tree and a canopy of bougainvillea. The clientele is mostly Greek, and the proprietor greets Maia with a kiss on both cheeks, nods to Tonio, and shows them to a table.

Tonio holds the chair for Maia. "You will let me order, yes?" she asks. "Kostos makes a fine lamb stew."

"That sounds fine. Thank you." Loosen up, Tonio. "Nice spot."

She orders a bottle of red wine from Crete and tomato and cucumber salads. Kostos brings the wine and pours two glasses. She lifts her glass and touches his.

"To adventure," she says.

"Adventure?" he replies. "Is that what we're here to discuss?"

A pause. "Tell me something about your work. I don't mean the cataloging. That's clear enough, but I am sure you have another interest. You spoke about the tholos tombs at Mycenae."

He explains about the Archaeology Department at Penn and his dissertation, how it focuses on the idea that the tholos tombs may be a guide to the development of Mycenaean settlement from the north into the Peloponnese and how most histories ignore the role of the tombs in describing an accurate chronicle of their movements. Maia listens intently, without interrupting.

Tonio takes a sip of wine. "It's difficult work, actually, because I have to do a lot of traveling and the funding is, well, minimal. So I have been working at Mycenae because of the rich supply of tombs, where I can measure, seeing the differences between sizes and designs. I'm really just at the beginning of the work."

Maia looks at him and then, "What is it about the tombs especially that captured your attention?"

"Strange that you should ask," he replies. "I was sitting one day in the largest tomb at Mycenae, on a day when there were no tourists around, just sitting at the center of the circle, when it came to me that here was this perfection of design, carved out of a hill by what is always thought of as a violent warlike culture with no philosophical or spiritual record to speak of, who made this memorial to the dead with such care and precision. Why? I wanted to know. So I guess it's more than an archeological exercise. I suppose that's why it was such a blow when I was forced to leave and come to Athens."

Their lamb stew arrives, and they eat mostly in silence. Tonio notices that she doesn't touch her wine, wondering, but not willing to ask. When the table is cleared, Maia seems to be listening to the music, but then begins to speak.

"Do you know that there was an earthquake near Ephesus four days ago?"

"No, was it a bad one? I mean, there seem to be earthquakes in Turkey weekly."

She nods. "This one was not bad, but what was interesting is that just outside of the ancient site, about three miles north, the ground shook enough to open a hole in a hillside and a good friend from the area went there and looked. She reported back that it appears that there might be a tholos tomb."

Tonio nods. "We know there were settlements up and down the coast there, and I learned just yesterday that Samos may prove fruitful as well." He hesitates, and just as he's about to say something, Kostos comes to the table to see what they will have next.

Maia smiles. "Kostos, the stew was beautiful. Tonio, would you like something else?"

"No, not for me." He says to Kostos, "The stew was wonderful."

Kostos asks, "Maia, how does it go with you?

Maia looks at Tonio and up at Kostos. "I'm fine, Kostos. Thank you for asking."

Kostos says to Tonio. "You must be careful young man . . ."

"Kostos," Maia speaks sharply. "This young man and I are talking business, nothing more."

Kostos puts a hand on his heart. "I am sorry Maia. It is not my place." He leans down and kisses her cheek. "Please accept this little dinner from me, and I hope to see you soon," and he leaves before she can say anything.

Maia says, "Kostos is like a father to me, fussing. He worries, thinking I work too hard."

"Do you?"

Maia stands up. "Let us walk."

Walking back toward the Agora, Maia leads the way to a small park and finds a bench. They sit, and for a minute are silent, watching traffic on the avenue. Tonio begins, "Before Kostos came to the table I was going to ask you why your friend did not explore further."

"She is too old to do more, but she called my mother, who set this project in motion. I want to ask you how long is your museum work?

"Until the end of August when I have to get back to the States. Why?"

Maia is silent, watching a couple walk by arm in arm. "If that is a tholos tomb, undiscovered, we have to explore it before the authorities find it." She stops.

"Because?"

"Because there may be things hidden in it, things of great value that must not fall into the wrong hands."

Tonio takes a breath. "I see, but usually the only things in a tholos tomb are bones and perhaps some sacred objects part of a burial. Very seldom anything truly valuable. No gold masks."

Maia smiles. "No, we're not grave robbers or fortune hunters. But there are other kinds of things that might be there."

"Such as?"

Maia is silent for a minute. Then, as if she has decided something, she turns to Tonio and begins. "In my time doing my doctorate at the Sorbonne, Dan Brown's book The DaVinci Code came out and we all had a good time reading it and discussing and eventually mocking the whole notion. And since most of it was set in Paris, we also found the guide markers and pretended to follow them and even one time gathered at the Louvre pyramid and chanted a Latin miserere until the guards told us to leave. Anyway, although we knew or thought we knew that there was nothing truly sacred in his book, when I got home to Crete and told my parents something of our goings-on, they were upset. They said that such mocking is dangerous, not because Brown's book was important, but because some of the content, if seriously studied, will bring great change and that it is best not to do any more mocking behavior. I was young and knew very little about things esoteric and spiritual."

Maia stops, seeming to wait for Tonio to say something, but he doesn't. She continues. "My parents live in what was once a small monastery. It was known locally as The Brotherhood of the Three Marys. The monks' scholarly work was trying to identify and separate the three Marys in the gospel accounts so as to prove that the Mary who was nearly stoned for adultery was not Mary Magdalene, but that she was the Mary close to Jesus and equal to the disciples in his eyes. And further that Jesus spoke to Mary of his deepest concerns and thoughts."

Tonio raises a finger. "Didn't Pope Francis some time ago declare Magdalene equal to the disciples, at least in the Roman Church?"

Maia nods. "Yes, he did and much of that decision came out of work done in Ephesus by various groups who claim she never left there and never went to live in a cave in France. It was thought, it seems, that both Greek and Roman sentiments changed about Magdalene as this century took hold and Francis, as a more daring Jesuit, decided to elevate her."

"So that's good, right? And what has that to do with the tomb? I mean, the tomb would have been constructed at least a thousand years before the time of Jesus. I'm not a very religious person and I don't see what more needs to be uncovered about her, unless of course you think she's buried in Ephesus."

Maia suddenly doubles over, seemingly in pain, then sits up and looks around. "Tonio, can you get me a taxi? This has been a long and stressful day."

Tonio, suddenly frightened, stands up. Holding out his hand, Maia takes it, stands up, and they walk out to the street, where Tonio hails a taxi and, opening the door, holds her arm as she climbs in.

She looks up, smiles, and says, "Can I email you?" They exchange email addresses, he shuts the door, and she is gone.

It's near midnight when he gets to his room. He undresses, crawls into bed, and stares at the ceiling. What just happened? What did the pith helmet faculty guy mean by "unwell" and Kostos mean about taking it easy with her, as if he was a date? And what was all this about an earthquake and Magdalene?

Lunch is arranged.

Subject: Tonight, and Mary
Tonio. Thank you for tonight You have been
very good. By the way, "Tonio" is not usually
followed by an English name like Fletcher.
How did that come about? Your darker skin
and those dark eyes suggest Italy. Yes?

But to the point, I would like to finish our
conversation. Are you free for lunch?
If so, suggest a time. Maia

Subject: Tonight, Mary, and Lunch
Lunch is fine. We break at Noon.
Meet at the South gate?
As to Tonio, my mother's heritage
is both English and Italian and when
I was born I had a head of very black
hair and dark eyes, and since my
professor father is a Thomas Mann
specialist and one of his favorite
short stories is titled "Tonio Kroger"
that became my name.
I hope you are feeling better . . .
Tonio

Subject: Lunch and Talk
Noon at the South gate is good.
Yes, I am feeling fine. Maia

Subject: Lunch and Talk
So that you are forewarned, my
questions will be along the lines
of Can you discuss what this is
about? And is this particular tomb
significant or do we look for others?
Tonio

Subject: Lunch and Talk
To your questions: yes and perhaps.
Maia

GATE NUMBER
THREE

AS ARRANGED, they meet at the South gate at noon. Maia leads the way a short distance to a cafe, where they avoid the crowded street floor and go upstairs to a cool and quiet room and table.

"This is nice," Tonio says. "I'm in the habit of buying lunch from the street venders and . . ."

"Sneaking into the theater," Maia smiles.

"True, but I think of it as a shortcut. I work for the Acropolis these days. They owe me. And after all, I found you there."

Maia actually blushes at this and studies the menu. "Are you coming up to me? she asks.

"Coming up? Oh, I see, you mean coming on. Perhaps I should explain. When you gathered the group around you and started talking, your arms seemed to me to float in the air, unjointed, as if you were, well, dancing. It was mesmerizing. Do you dance?"

Maia puts the menu down. "I did as a child, but when we moved to Crete from Thessaloniki there was no opportunity. I am sorry about the 'coming on' remark. I am perhaps too wary. Paris is full of eager men, some of whom do not take no for an answer."

"Well," Tonio says, "you must make a better effort not to be so mesmerizing."

"I shall try." She sticks out her tongue. "There."

Tonio puts his hand on his heart. "I'm devastated."

Maia laughs.

After lunch, sipping espresso, Maia says, "I feel I can trust you with more about what is going on and why I am 'coming on to you' this way, as it were."

"Good. I'm listening."

She takes another sip. "First, I need to explain last night. I had an operation in Paris this spring to remove a small tumor in my intestine, but it appears they were too conservative, and it has returned. I will have another surgery in Crete soon, but first I must go to Ephesus."

"But surely the operation is more important," Tonio said. "You must . . ."

"No," Maia interrupts. "There are reasons why I must go to Ephesus now, next week in fact. The discovery of the tomb will attract attention and there are those who will search it and if they find what may be hidden there, the result will be, or may be, well, a catastrophe."

"Why?" What do you think is there?"

"For a decade now, we have been certain that the text of what is called the Gospel of Mary, which is fragmented in the Nag Hammadi materials, was intentionally edited to leave out material that speaks to things Jesus told Mary about his ministry, about what he hoped would come from his teaching. In one critical verse in the present text, Mary asks how we are to see and understand his vision and he replies, 'You do not see through the soul nor through the spirit, but the mind that is between the two that is what sees the vision and it is . . .' and the rest is missing. We think the material was cut out because it has something to do with how Jesus saw what was to take place in forming a new religion from his teaching. What we want to find, if it exists, are the complete texts and learn what it says."

"OK, but why this place in particular?"

"That is a long story, but the short of it is that not far from the ancient city is a burial site called the Cave of the Seven Sleepers . . . and according to Christian belief, when Mother Mary and Magdalene fled Jerusalem after the storm surrounding the missing body of Jesus and the talk of resurrection, they went north and settled in Ephesus until their deaths . . . and that Magdalene, who lived longer, may be buried in the Cave of the Sleepers. To this day, women go to the fence surrounding the enclosure and leave notes and prayers on pieces of white cloth tied to the fence."

Tonio sits up straight in his chair. "Yes, I know. It's the same as at the shrine you spoke of about Antigone. There are the same white strips there. Do these women think Magdalene is present there in some way?"

"Yes, but not buried there."

"So, you think there might be something in the tomb because it is near this enclosure?"

"Exactly, and we know that the Sleepers Cave nearby has been searched again and again, looking for anything concerning Mary. And now, my mother says that the tomb will be discovered soon and we must be there first."

"And they can't go to Ephesus?"

"No, my father is disabled, and Mother cannot leave him, and the last of the monks is also too old to travel, much less deal with the tomb."

Silence. Tonio gazes out the window onto the street below, where life goes on in its busy, frantic way. Finally, he says, "And so, you would like me to go with you to excavate the tomb. Next week."

Maia lights up. "Why do you think you were in the theater the other day? You were sent."

"To my failed career as a professor of archaeology."

"No, to do something unimagined and perhaps much more important."

Tonio laughs. "Now you are coming up to me."

"Yes I am. Please." She puts her hand on his arm "You are needed. And if you do come, I will tell you how I know and why it will not be a fool's errand."

Tonio looks into Maia's eyes, which hold him fast. "You are either an angel or a devil."

"What does your heart say?"

"The former. I am lost."

"Or found."

After a nearly sleepless night, Tonio tells Jean-Marc that he is leaving. Angered at the loss of company, Jean-Marc swears curses upon Tonio's eternal soul. Daniel, surprised, is less angry but more perplexed and hurt. Director Templeton curses and threatens to call Tonio's advisor at Penn. Tonio apologizes, saying it's an emergency. Only Judith Diels is sympathetic, even encouraging, telling him not to worry, that tempers will cool over time, that she will deal with Templeton, who's afraid of her she says, and that she will try to find someone to take his place.

"After all," she says, "they pulled you away from your real work without apology."

Tonio thanks her and promises to keep her in the loop, as soon as he knows what's really going on.

Three days later, his necessities crammed into his backpack and all the money he had left in the bank converted to dollars (Maia's idea because the Turks love dollars), he sits by the South gate at three in the afternoon, reading an English version of an Ephesus guidebook. A picture-spread in it explains the myth of the Seven Sleepers who, as early Christians were pursued by angry pagans, fled to the caves and went to sleep, so it was written . . . and woke two hundred years later into a Christian world.

At the appointed hour Maia drives up in a camper.

He climbs in, looks around, and makes a low whistle. "Well, this is something. A rental?"

"Yes, for a month if needed, and if we're lucky we can take it as far as Crete. And if we find something, there are places to hide things. Do you have your passport?"

"Of course. What do you mean hide things?" he asked. "That sounds ominous."

"If we find anything of value, the Turkish authorities won't let us just make off with it. We'll have to smuggle it out."

Tonio has visions of spending the rest of his life in a Turkish prison, images of which cause chills. His mood shifts for a moment until Maia says, "With just you and me and this camper, we are holiday travelers driving down the coast from Troy and going to Samos to visit where Pythagoras was born. I even brought along some rings. My mother's idea. The Turks like married couples."

Tonio smiles. "Coming up to me again."

Maia laughs, puts the camper in gear, and heads for the high-way to Piraeus. "The fast boat leaves at six and, after a few island-stops, arrives in Samos in the morning. The ride should be smooth. The Mediterranean doesn't get angry until mid-August."

"You've been on the sea a lot?'

"Well, once you live in Crete, it happens that way. Flying is expensive, and the ships are part of the Greek way of life."

They soon find their way to the right ship and, because they are getting off last, they board quickly, followed by delivery trucks and cars for the near island stops. They find lounge chairs in the main stateroom and Maia falls asleep almost immediately. Tonio reads his Ephesus guide for a time and then sleeps, too, but wakes a little after six when the engines hum and vibrate into life, and they slowly leave the harbor for open water.

This journey, or interim, sets Tonio and Maia at ease with one another. The frantic few days up to this moment were behind them and for Tonio, there was nothing he could do now but look ahead and leave the Agora museum behind, never to return. For Maia, too, whatever lay ahead were days to be shared now with Tonio, whose skills were beyond hers and whatever was to take place was also beyond her strength, more so because her future was also uncertain—although last night on the phone her mother said, "It is as I told you Maia, just trust."

GATE NUMBER
FOUR

SUCH ARE their thoughts and the conversation flows accordingly in what they share now, that and whatever lies ahead. When they leave the last island stop and begin the last uninterrupted leg before reaching Samos, they have something to eat and then go up on deck, partly to get away from the blaring music, which Maia explains is a mix of rock and folk music called Laika. Up on deck the breeze and silence welcome them and the fading day, with a moon rising, says that all is well. Stars soon appear by the billions.

Maia surprises him by putting her arm under his, sheltering herself against the sea air. "You are like a tree," she says.

"Ah," he replies, "then I'll be silent like one."

"No, talk to me in tree-talk. What do you say, tree, out here where there are no roots or birds to make nests in your branches?"

"We trees are the greatest beings because the largest single organism on this planet is a stand of aspen hundreds of miles in diameter in Utah, all rooted together as a single tree."

"Is that true?"

"Partly. It's called Pando. Beautiful yellow leaves that vibrate in the breeze."

"Why is it one organism rather than single trees?"

"Because they have identical genetic markers and are joined together at the roots, as I said, and if one tree is sick, they all come to her aid and find a solution, a protection against attack."

"So that's what you're going to do."

"Yes. Doing, not going to. Putting your arm through mine is a start. So, don't let go."

"Why did you say 'partly?'"

"Ah, well, to be accurate, I also heard that really the world's largest organism is actually a giant mushroom in Oregon, that is almost five miles wide. But it's mostly underground."

"I prefer the Great Tree," and she grips a little tighter. After a time, Maia says, "I'm very tired. Can we sleep in the camper?"

"I don't see why not," he replies.

With a blast of its horn, the ship announces its approach to Samos, and wakes Tonio and Maia. With a shudder the boat's engine slips into reverse, and it inches slowly to the dock and is tied up. Maia and Tonio dress quickly and are ready when the gate opens, and vehicles begin to move. They drive slowly on to the quay and park in a waiting area to board the ferry to Kusadasi. It will be a short trip of less than an hour and, once there, they will pass through the Turkish authorities at the port of entry.

As they wait, Maia says, "It's best if you handle the talking in Kusadasi. As an American you will have an easier time. We Greeks do not fare well with the Turks, but in tourist season I do not worry about any trouble."

"Reminds me of a joke Jean-Marc told me. Greeks are really Turks trying to be Italians."

"Ha!" she bursts out and hits his arm. "Mind your manners, sir, there is truth only in the geography. Funny though. I'm sorry we won't have enough time to visit Samos, particularly the little harbor at Pythagorio, birthplace of Pythagoras. There are at least a dozen quaint cafes in a semicircle around the harbor wall, and it is so protected that even a great storm is not a danger."

"Perhaps when we return," Tonio says.

With that the ferry whistle blows and cars line up to board. Once aboard, they leave the camper and go to the bow. The morning sun is bright and the sky clear. Shielding her eyes, Maia takes a deep breath. "We should be early enough to avoid the big tourist ships. Ephesus has great appeal and there are church groups that follow the path of Saint John, whose grave is at Selcuk. There is also the Virgin Mary's little stone house in the hills above the temple site."

"Is there much left of the temple?"

"No, just one partial column with a stork nest on the top."

"That's a nice touch."

Maia smiles and turns around to avoid the sun. Tonio turns as well and asks, "How do you feel?"

"I feel better. Getting out of Athens air and the bus rides, not to mention the chattering and singing kids. But they were nice, in fact, well-behaved." Maia's mention of the tour group brings Templeton to mind and Tonio wonders if he has contacted Professor Burnside at Penn, and if so, where things stand.

As Kusadasi comes into view, they can see that the cruise ships have yet to arrive, except for one at anchor outside the harbor.

"We are fortunate," Maia says as they return to the camper. "Have your passport ready."

"Should we wear our rings?" Tonio quips as he pockets his passport. "We forgot to ask the ferry captain to make us official."

Maia smiles. "The rings are for the exit, that is if we have something to hide. If we don't it won't be such a happy wedding trip."

The line of cars begins to move, and soon enough they reach the line of officials, where they get out. While their passports are being stamped, one official walks around the camper, opens the passenger side sliding door and peers inside but doesn't touch anything, and closes the door. The official with his stamp says to Tonio in clipped English. "Have a pleasant time in Turkey, Sir and Madam."

Before getting back in the camper, Tonio asks, "Would you like me to drive while you hold the map?"

Maia says, "I know the way to Selcuk, our first stop, but after that you drive. We'll need the map to get to the cave." They head out along the quay, up the winding road from the harbor.

Once out of Kusadasi into the countryside, Maia says, "We stop first in Selcuk to visit a good friend of my parents. Her name is Filiz. She is the one who after the earthquake went to the Sleepers Cave at my mother's direction to see if there was any damage there and spotted the hole or damage to the hillside. It was she who called my parents, excited that it might mean something, either good or bad, and that we should investigate. Also, I would like to stop, have a bath, and change for our work."

"Good idea," Tonio responds. "So, you said tourists come to follow John and visit the house of the Virgin. Is there interest here in Magdalene?"

"Not very much in Turkey. The believers here are mostly old women who keep to the Christian faith even as Turkey moves to Islam, or at least as many have. There is such trouble and conflict, although Erdogan keeps a tight grip on the country, so it is not like Egypt where the Coptic Christians are attacked, and the government does little to protect them."

"Religion causes wars upon wars upon wars," Tonio says.

"It is so." Turning off the main road, they slow, enter a street lined with modest homes. After a short distance, Maia points to one and says, "Here we are. Filiz is expecting us."

The door opens to reveal an old woman with a beaming face draped in a shawl. She embraces Maia and says in Greek, "You are thin, Maia. How is it with you?'

Maia replies in English. "And you Filiz, you look no different.

This is my friend Tonio. He knows all about tholos tombs and has come to help, as I told you."

Filiz takes Tonio's hand in both of hers, "Blessings to you, my boy. You are welcome." She turns to Maia, "Such a handsome young man, Maia. Where did you find him?"

"Working in the Agora, Filiz. I will tell you all about it."

"Come in. Come in," and they go into the small house, decorated in a mixed collection of Turkish fabrics and rugs, with more contemporary furniture and paintings.

"You have a beautiful home, Filiz," Tonio says.

"Thank you . . . I'm sorry, what is your name again?"

Maia laughs, "It is Tonio."

"What kind of name is that? Are you Italian?"

Before Tonio can answer, Maia says, "That is another story Filiz, for another time. Before we move on to the sleeper caves, I would love to have a bath and a change."

"Yes, yes, of course. You will both want to wash up. I have prepared a small lunch and some food to take with you. Will you be coming back here this evening?"

"Thank you, no. We have the camper and will sleep there. The less movement in and out of the area, the better."

Filiz puts a finger to her temple. "Yes, that is wise."

Bathed, changed, and fed, Maia and Tonio, with a basket of food, pull away from the house, with Filiz waving in the doorway. Maia holds the map and points Tonio to the east and after no more than three miles she points to a dirt road on the left. They drive only a few hundred yards before entering an acre or more of densely packed bamboo trees. Maia points to an opening with car tracks, just large enough for one vehicle.

Tonio pulls in and shuts the engine off. "OK," he says.

"Welcome to the Bamboo Resort and Spa. I for one could use a massage after my bath."

"Be serious now, Tonio. This could be dangerous."

"I know. You might remember for the future that humor is how I hide my feelings in anxious moments."

GATE NUMBER
FIVE

THEY WALK toward the hill, which Tonio estimates to be about four or five hundred feet high. They reach a path, and Maia turns to the right where they see a serious looking chain link fence. On it are small white strips tied to the links.

"Just like the fence at the theater."

"Yes," Maia says.

When they reach the fence, Tonio is surprised. Rather than a cave, as he had imagined, the area is open, with carved burial alcoves, and evidence of pilings which must have at one time supported a roof. "It's not really a cave at all," he says.

"No. The theory is that it began as a rather primitive cave for the deposit of bones, but by the Later Roman Period the area was improved to accommodate the wealthy and well-connected. The story about the seven sleepers is dated around 250 CE, and the story goes that seven young Christians escaped from the pagan prison of Emperor Decius and came here when it was a real cave, where they hid. The legend is that they slept for two hundred years and woke to find the whole world Christian."

"Ah, and if they had slept for another five hundred years the world would be Muslim. So, you were saying that this area has been thoroughly searched for evidence of burials, Magdalene in particular?"

"Yes, by grave robbers as well as the faithful, and it has been picked clean, so Filiz says."

What do these little strips say, I wonder?

"Prayers for loved ones, cures from illness, forgiveness in general. It was thought by the early Church Fathers that by linking Magdalene to the woman taken in adultery that women could more easily approach her with prayers rather than to the Virgin, who was perfect and might not understand or forgive."

"Makes sense," Tonio replies, "but not so much for Mary's reputation." He turns away from the fence. "Where's the hole in the hillside?"

Maia starts down the path. "This way. Filiz said it is about forty meters past the driveway, and about three or four meters up the slope."

"Well, if it's a tholos, four meters would be very small for one, that is, if the cave-in was from the top, but if from the side, then the integrity of the structure might be very shaky."

Pacing off the distance from the drive, they see nothing, but after another few meters Maia points and says, "There." And further up the slope is a ragged hole more than a meter wide. On all fours Tonio works slowly up the slope, several times jamming his knees into the ground to feel for some give, until he reaches the hole. Taking a flashlight from his belt, he lies down and shines the light into the hole.

After a minute, he sits up and says, "Well it's either another cave or maybe, just maybe, a tholos."

"Why maybe?"

"All I can see now is the dirt and some stones from the cave-in. I can't see more of the cave floor, or whether the stones are finished rather than natural. What we need is a stronger light, and I have one in my pack."

"I'll get it. Stay there." Maia goes back to the camper, while Tonio tries a get a better view without falling in.

Back with the light, Maia takes a few steps up the slope and Tonio slips down to meet her, takes the light, and moves back up to the opening. This time he catches a glimpse of a row of carved stones rising from a flat clear dirt floor.

He sits up and turning around and catching his breath gives a thumbs up. "I'm not sure it's a tholos yet, until I can clear a few stones around this hole, but there's no doubt it's a formal cave, man-made for certain." He slides down and when he stands up Maia slips into his arms and gives him a hug.

She says into his shoulder, "Thank you, Tonio. Thank you so much for doing this."

Tonio, flashlight in one hand and the other arm around her says, "I wouldn't have missed it for the world. This is really very cool."

As the day grows late, Tonio has made another examination and they are back in the camper. Maia is resting and Tonio is making notes. After a few more minutes, he whispers, "Maia?"

She turns. "Is everything all right?"

"Yes, fine, but we need something. In order to work with this hole in this position, which can't be very stable, we need to spread the weight for going down into the space as wide as possible. So, if I tie our rope to a tree up the slope and we place a long wide board close to the hole, so as to spread the weight over a larger area, we should be OK, or at least a little more secure. So, where can we get a board?

Maia sits up and with that gesture of her arm that gives Tonio shivers, she covers a yawn and says, "I'll call Filiz and see what she can do." An hour later, Filiz arrives with an ironing board. Tonio ties the rope to a tree and places the board just above the top section of the hole. Then tying a series of knots in the rope for foot and hand holds, he drops the rope into the hole. It's dark now, so they go back to the van and open the bundle of food from Filiz, which even includes a jar of a rich red wine.

After they eat, Maia goes off into the grove. She returns after a few minutes and says that she's exhausted. They roll out their sleeping bags. Maia turns away, removes her shoes and slacks, and slips into her bag. Tonio follows suit and crawls into his bag. After a moment or two, Maia turns to Tonio and gently kisses him on the cheek. "Thank you, Toni-oo."

Tonio says good-night and turns onto his side. He feels a rising desire but doesn't act on it. It was sisterly, he tells himself. But he likes the sound of Toni-oo, a new sound, and soon enough falls asleep.

Tonio is awakened in the night by what he thinks is an owl or other sort of bird, but soon realizes it is Maia. She's moaning in her sleep. Now she turns almost violently in the bag and sits up.

Tonio also sits up. "What is it?"

"Pain," she says. "Did I wake you?"

"You were moaning. Is there anything I can do?"

There is a pill bottle in the compartment in the dash."

Tonio slips out of his bag and goes around to the passenger door. The pills are in a small white bag. He gives it to her with a bottle of water.

Maia takes two pills and draws her knees to her chest, with her head down.

Not knowing what if anything to do, Tonio rubs her back slowly and then strokes her hair.

"Oh, that's nice," she says. After a few minutes she unwinds and slowly slips back in her bag.

"Pain killers?"

"Mmm."

"Powerful?"

"Mmm."

"Sorry."

A hand comes to his cheek. "I should not drink wine," she says, "but I thought we needed to celebrate a bit."

He puts his hand over hers. "Nothing to celebrate yet. Maybe nothing down there but snakes waiting for some idiot to drop in."

She withdraws her hand and laughs. "Thanks, now I'll dream of Harrison Ford and something Jones."

"Indiana."

She slips further into her bag and murmurs, "Yes, Indiana . . . where is that?" and is asleep.

He slides into his bag. "In the middle of nowhere," he says and strokes her hair for a while longer.

The next day breaks humid, with dark clouds. Tonio sits up and watches Maia sleep. Easing out of his bag, he pulls on a tee and his shorts. His face itches and he feels the stubble. He decides to let it grow, not shave. He would look older, cutting into the few years between them. He had felt something there last night, a closeness that gave him hope, and then, just as suddenly, the pain of uncertainty. What is her body doing to her? She seems hopeful, but is that just to ease his mind, focusing on the search instead? Pressure on his bladder ends his reverie and as quietly as he can he opens the side door, but Maia wakes.

"Morning," he says. "Sorry to wake you, but I have to go."

She sits up, the bag slipping down revealing her breasts and below that a scar down to her waist. She stretches but doesn't cover up.

Tonio looks away. "It's going to be cloudy, maybe rain . . . could complicate things."

Maia slips on her shirt. "Will the rain weaken the hill?"

"No, not unless we have a long downpour. It might just make things slippery. I'll be back in a minute, or maybe a little more," and he reaches for the roll of toilet paper.

Meanwhile Maia takes another pill with a sip of water and figures out how the small camp stove works. When Tonio returns, she smiles and hands him a steaming cup. "Have some coffee. Sugar?"

"Wow, that's great. No, no sugar." Taking the cup, "Thanks."

Within the hour, now nearly eight, they are at the hill, everything in place. Tonio climbs up to the hole and gives the rope a good tug. He sits, his legs in the hole. He makes sure the light is secure in his belt and turning, says, "Be careful coming up, not to dislodge anything. This hole is frayed around the edges."

"I'll be careful. You too."

"Right." He holds the rope and turning, eases into the hole, and finding a knot in the rope below lets himself down, knot by knot, until he reaches the pile of dirt and stone. He steps to the open floor, takes the light, and examines his surroundings.

Maia's head appears above. "What do you see?"

"It's a beehive tomb all right," he replies.

"There are bees?"

"No, there are several different designs of these tholos tombs. This is one of the so-called beehive designs, the way the rows of stone rise and close at the top. This one looks quite well built, which is why the whole thing didn't collapse when the quake shook it." He looks around until he finds the frame of the entrance and is sure it would be impossible to dig out through there.

Maia says, "Do you see anything else?"

"Not yet, but there's the usual side room, where the bones of an earlier burial were placed when a new body was interred. Just a second." Tonio shines his light the anteroom and goes in. It is clean, no sign of bones or anything else. He goes back and looks up at Maia.

I'm sorry Maia, I don't see anything else. It's empty."

"But there has to be. My mother said to Filiz, "Search for a tomb near the Sleeper Cave. There will be something important but hidden." She said well-hidden."

"How would your mother know that?"

"She has a very vivid dream life and many examples that come to pass. She called me in Paris and told me that I was ill before I even had a symptom.

Tonio says, "Well, all right. I can trust that, but I don't know how something can be hidden in here."

"Why not?"

He thinks. "Well, the designs of these tombs are always geometrically precise. The main tomb is always a perfect circle, and this one looks perfect, but I'll check and see if any stones look to be dislodged."

Above, Maia can see the light moving slowly around the tomb, once, twice, and more, moving higher each time.

Tonio says, "There is some displacement of the perfection of how stones were fitted. I'll check the anteroom, which is always uniform."

"Why such perfection?"

"Mostly proper reverence, we think, but since there's so little writing in the Mycenaean record, we don't know more than that."

Tonio returns to the anteroom. "Funny but I feel a lightness."

"Tonio, what? You see a light?"

He steps back into the tomb and looks up. "No not a light, but a lightness, a feeling."

"Mother said there might be a glow."

He flicks off his flashlight. He looks back into the anteroom. "No glow or light. I said a lightness. I'll go back in."

With that, Tonio moves into the anteroom again, this time

focusing on shape. He carefully paces the floor. "Aha!" he yells.

"What?"

"It's not uniform. The anteroom door is not centered, which may mean that the wall on this side could be false." Could you see if there's anything in the camper toolbox that might be useful for prying a rock?"

"Where would the toolbox be?"

"Probably in the back. There should be a panel in the floor."

While waiting, Tonio examines the wall. He begins feeling the stones from the top down and finds a few that are loose, perhaps from the quake, but perhaps also from careless or hurried construction. After all, if someone disturbed this tomb more than a thousand years after it was built, the workmanship could not be as perfect.

Maia returns and calls, "I found a short spade. The 4-way thing for tightening tire nuts won't help, right?"

"Right. Drop the spade. I found a few loose stones in the anteroom and the spade should help. Thanks."

"Watch out!" and she drops the spade.

"Got it." Standing under the hole he feels some drops. "Is it raining?"

"A little."

"Stay dry if you can." He takes the spade into the anteroom. Loosening a few stones near the top, he is able to remove three and then two from the second row. Shining the light into the space, he sees there is another wall, the original. He can't see anything more and begins removing more stones, knowing now that he isn't weakening the integrity of the whole structure. With four rows of stones removed at the center, he can peer into the space.

There on the floor are two amphoras, with handles, in the Classical mode. Each is perhaps eight inches wide and two feet high. Tonio's heart races. "Jesus Christ," he mutters.

"Maia!" He leaves the anteroom. Looking up, her face is partly hidden by his own Phillies baseball cap. "There are two amphoras behind the wall. Classical design."

"Oh, Tonio! Oh God! What do we do next?"

"Let me think. I can't disassemble the whole wall."

"You can't reach them?"

"No, that's the problem, I would have to take a whole section of the wall out." He thinks. "Or, since they have handles, we could hook a handle and raise them that way." Pause. "But if they're heavy, that would be dangerous."

Maia, says, "Well if you did hook onto a handle and tried to lift and it was too heavy, we would have to take the wall out."

"We need a fishing pole."

"Sorry."

"Ah! OK, what we need is a strip of cloth at least five feet long or some string or a piece of our rope and then take a spoon and bending both ends up, tie to one end and I'll try to hook a handle end with the other."

"I'll be back," Maia says and is gone. In the meantime, Tonio works on a few more stones and manages to create another foot of opening.

Maia returns. "Here," and tosses down a strip of pale blue cloth with a spoon attached.

Tonio picks up the spoon and looks up at Maia. "This is from your dress, isn't it?"

"What better sacrifice to make?" she says. "Will you need help?"

"No. I don't want you to try to come down. Besides, you will need to pull up each amphora. Oh, by the way, do not, no matter how curious you are, try to open one."

"Why?"

"Whatever is in them may be two thousand years old at least and fragile and exposing it to the air would be a disaster."

"Yes, I see. Oh, Tonio I hope there are scrolls. Mother said so."

"Amazing woman, your mother."

Tonio bends the spoon into an S shape wide enough to grasp a handle. With the light in one hand and the fabric in the other, he lets the spoon down. When it stops spinning, he eases it onto one of the handles and gently pulls. The amphora moves, swinging a little, but it feels light enough to lift. Holding the fabric firmly, he hooks his light into his belt and then hand over hand raises the amphora until he can grab the other handle.

Letting out his breath, he holds the amphora and goes into the outer room and holds it up for Maia to see. She puts a hand to her mouth but says nothing. Tonio puts the amphora down on its side and, getting an ear as close to it as possible, he gently rolls it. There is the sound of an object or objects moving inside.

"There's something solid in there. It's either a pouch of gold coins or a scroll, I'm sure. But I don't hear coins."

"Good," Maia says.

"I'll get the other," and he goes back and repeats the process, and puts the second to the same test. In this one he hears a more distinct thump when he rolls the jar.

"Maia, I'll attach each one at a time to the rope, and you can pull them up. Then we'll figure out how to hide them securely. I'm also thinking that it might be a good idea for me to put the wall back together, in case others come along and start a search for us grave robbers. It won't look the same, but it may not raise suspicions. I'll also see if I can erase my footprints. Maybe after we raise the jars you could break a branch to make a crude broom and drop it in here."

The amphoras are safely raised, and after an hour's work, the wall is reasonably repaired. Tonio sweeps the floor, climbs the rope, and pulls himself over the ironing board and up the slope to untie the rope from the tree. He sits under the shelter of the leaves for a few minutes, catching his breath. Maia comes from the camper, with the Phillies cap low on her brow, holds out a glass of wine.

"Can I induce you to come down, so I can give you a well-deserved hug? And if that is not incentive enough, there is this glass of wine."

"It will take both offers to get me up, but I'll try." Easing himself up, he works his way down the hill, around the hole and to the glass, which he empties in one swallow and then receives his hug, which turns into a kiss.

"You taste delicious," he says."

"And you, sir, taste of sweat and tombs."

"Well, let's hope that what we have are not church records or more letters to the early Church Fathers."

"Seriously, my heroic wonder, if what we hope is true, it will be that Magdalene is taking issue with Paul and the later so-called church fathers. I have made sandwiches and put out some dry clothes that I found when I took everything from your backpack, so I could hide our treasures in it."

"Well-padded I trust?"

"I think so, yes."

"Well enough to pass inspection?"

"I doubt that. We will just have to be friendly, I think."

After they have something to eat, Maia goes over what's to come next. First, they must return the now famous ironing board to Filiz, and then take the ferry over to Samos. From there they hopefully will be able to take a ship via Naxos, Thira, and finally to Crete.

"May I assume you don't want to go back to Athens?" she asks.

"You may. That part of my life appears to be over, and my curiosity about our discovery is for the moment what interests me. That and meeting this remarkable mother of yours with her uncanny dreaming. I still have a hard time with all that has happened to this point."

Maia says, "She is remarkable. But there was also a clue. In the Gospel of Magdalene in the Nag Hammadi materials, there is a reference to her revelation about Jesus and his concern about a religion in his name. My mother has been piecing together many sources and in the process having dreams about their meaning."

"Still," Tonio says, "it does appear that she has a mysterious mind that one could learn much from."

"It is true and my great sorrow is that as a young and arrogant youth, I rebelled from her teaching and doubted her. But when she warned me about my illness and now this, I mean to put myself in her care and to pay attention."

"Is it she who will work with whatever it is we have found?"

"She will have a part, but fortunately, as I think I mentioned, we have with our family one last member of the Brotherhood of the Marys and if we do have ancient scrolls, he will be the expert."

As they are cleaning up, Tonio asks, "What happens to the camper?"

"I hope we can leave it on the dock in Crete to go back to Athens. Or some tourists will arrive and rent it to tour Knossos."

Maia spends much of the afternoon on her cell gathering ship schedules out of Samos to Crete. As it turns out, with the weekend arriving, no ship is scheduled until Monday. That leaves them forty-eight hours of leisure, some of which will be spent with Filiz. Then there will be a night in Samos, which means another call to find a room on the island. That taken care of, they recover the very wet ironing board from the hill and tie it to the roof of the camper. They agree that even though a visit to Ephesus would be educational, they don't dare leave the camper unattended.

The rest of the afternoon passes quietly, and after a small supper, they undress and slip into their bags. As he had the night before, Tonio strokes Maia's hair until he thinks she's asleep.

He takes his hand away and says softly, almost to himself, "I do love you, you know."

As he is turning, she says, "Why?"

Startled, he says, "Why do I love you?"

"Yes."

"I told you once in Athens that you are very mysterious to me. I had always thought that love is something that grows slowly between two people, when they have been friends for a long time. You know, based on mutual interests, ideas, plans for their future. Now you come along, and the difference is startling."

Maia is now watching him carefully. She says, "And you think perhaps we don't have those things, I mean interests, ideas in common?"

"Of course, that's obvious now, I think, but they were not the basis of my attraction to you."

"Which was what?"

"Are you fishing now?"

"Fishing?"

"I mean, do you want to know, really, why I'm attracted to you or . . ."

"I want to know, yes."

"All right," he says bracing his head with his left hand. "I know it sounds strange to say so, but first, it's the way you move, but more, the way you are in the world. You were in the theater, that day, moving those kids around, and it was as if you had some power over them, but not just as a grown-up telling them what to do and what to think. It was, well, influence, not command. And then, and tell me if I'm wrong here, after that there was a need in you that surprised me. What exactly that is I'm not sure. I felt needed in a way I've never known before. And respected, too."

Tonio looks at her more closely and sees in her large dark eyes something profoundly sad, as if this moment is somehow not for her what it is for him. He smoothes her hair with his free hand

and she closes her eyes and seems to let go, sinking back into her sleeping bag.

She opens her eyes. "There is a need, Tonio, and you do fill it. Yes." He keeps stroking the hair behind her ear until he knows this time that she has fallen asleep. He wants to explore her response further, but it will have to wait. By then he too is relaxed and sleepy. He turns down the lantern and lies back.

Sometime during the night Tonio wakes to the sound of rain. He turns onto his back and lies listening to the sound of water falling among the bamboo leaves and on the roof of the camper. It's a welcome sound, after these weeks of heat, sun, and dry wind. Looking over his shoulder, he sees that Maia is not in her bag. He feels for his light and shines it around. She isn't there. His watch reads 1:15. Perhaps she needed to relieve herself. He waits some minutes, listening to the rain, but she doesn't return. He slips out of his bag, leaves the camper, and walks over to the path. She isn't there. The rain is steady, but not heavy. It is cool on his skin. He scans the slope above but sees nothing. He walks along the path, but after a few yards, he stops. She wouldn't go up to the cave. He calls her name softly but there is no reply.

He goes back down the path and then walks a bit down the road. The rain runs down his face, and his boxer shorts are quickly soaked. Off to the side, in the field, he sees what might be a figure lying on the matted grass. The light reveals Maia lying on her back. She seems to be fused into the earth, sunk nearly halfway into the ground, as if being drawn down. Tonio nearly runs to her, as if to pull her back, but instead he climbs slowly through the fence and walks quietly to her. He clicks the light off.

She is on her back, naked, her eyes closed, one arm thrown back above her head, the other over her eyes. Tonio stands for a few moments looking at her. Her small breasts are stretched white against the darkness of her neck and shoulders. Below her navel the scar runs down into her dark pubic hair. He moves closer and kneels. Her arm drops down to her side, but she doesn't open her eyes. She sighs.

"Join me, Tonio," she says "The rain feels like a gift from the gods." He lies down next to her.

"I woke up and you weren't there," he says. "With the rain, I didn't think you'd be outside."

"Mmm, it's all right, I'm fine," she says. "I'm washing the dirt off."

Tonio raises himself on his elbow and looks at her. He reaches out his left hand and touches her stomach, then runs a finger down the scar, along its length. She shudders and then lies still. Her hand finds his thigh and then touches his wet shorts.

She laughs. "Get out of those," she says. Tonio hesitates, wanting for a moment to hide his growing desire, but he slides them off and then turns on his side again. Once more he touches the scar.

She turns her head and looks at him. Her hand finds his erection. It's like an electric shock. "Lie back," she whispers. On his back, with the rain hitting his face, Tonio closes his eyes and feels her slow, exploring caresses. She leans over and kisses his chest. He raises his head and kisses her wet hair. She gently pushes him back. She wipes hair from his eyes. "Be very still, she whispers. "Try to be very still."

She raises herself and swings her right leg over his body. Her hand gently guides him inside her, but just barely. She moves slightly, suspended above him. Then, very slowly, she allows herself to be filled, lowering her body to his hips and then to his chest, where she lies still again. They stay that way for some minutes, the rain filling up the spaces where their bodies are folded together. Tonio breathes deeply, throbbing inside her, trying to hold himself still. Instinctively, his groin lifts slightly and falls back. He moans.

Maia smooths his cheek, kissing him, and whispers "Be very still."

Tonio can feel her body pressing backwards against his hardness. The pressure is steady, with only a suggestion of movement. She pushes herself up, her hands on his shoulders, and arches her back. Her breathing grows deeper and faster, the movement more pronounced, until he feels her shudder and then shudder again. A small cry escapes, and then she lowers her body to his again and is still.

Tonio can feel his own release coming then, and his body tenses. "Oh, God," he whispers, "I'm coming."

She holds him firmly. "Yes," she whispers in his ear, and his body releases. He can feel the wet grass and the rain and her weight on him. When the spasms stop, she says, "Wait, wait, my sweet god." They lie together for a long time, and then she slowly rolls off and lies on her back. The rain is steady and a little cooler now, chilling.

He looks down at her again. She seems so small, vulnerable, not at all the tough, determined woman he has spent these past days with. Somehow the scar is a tear in her armor. He kisses her. She closes her eyes, her chest rising and falling. He touches the scar again, this time with his lips. "Are you going to tell me about this?" he says, resting his cheek on her stomach.

Her hands smooth his hair. "As I mentioned in Athens, it was two years ago, in Paris. The call came from my mother, worried. I was having intestinal problems and a CAT scan showed a colon blockage. They took a big piece out. Twenty centimeters or so. That's the scar. A malignant piece. Aggressive, was the term they used. Didn't get it all, they said. This March I had some more scraping done, in the intestinal wall, and they may have gotten that. They suggest conventional therapies, but I said no."

"But there must be . . ."

Maia touches his arm. "No, it's all right, Tonio. I'm not going to let modern medicine have this body for their experiments in delay and more delay. I came back to Crete to be with my family, to help with my father, and to do something worth doing with my life. As soon as I left the hospital, I knew I would not go back to Paris. That part of my life is over. It was all cancerous. The Sorbonne was a hospital, too, a place for the sick and injured, where professors cut and drained and proscribed. My life there began to look all the same. Back in Crete I began to find real healing, real love and real life again. My mother took over and began to use the old remedies. It may be too late, but I feel I have my life back for a time. When this happened, when we were told that something important would happen in Ephesus, I knew I must be a part of it. Mother thinks it is all related, of course. She told me to go to Athens. There I would find help."

She looks up at Tonio, whose face in the rain looks as if it is running with tears. His hair and growing beard drips onto her stomach. She touches his face. "I did not know that I would find such strength in you, Tonio. You have been exactly what was needed, in many ways."

"But what are you going to do?" he asks.

"I am doing it, putting my faith in what I must do, making of my life something important and useful. It is what you too are doing now, yes?"

"Yes, but I have also found you now. What has been important for me in this time has been you, who you are, doing this together."

Maia looks at him and then turns her head away. "In Athens I felt somehow you could save me, make a different ending, and I ached for you. I don't know if you can pull me out of this collapsed body of mine, can you? I'm trapped in here and I won't get out until it just goes away."

Tonio stares into the darkness and feels the chill of the rain on his body. Maia seems to shiver, too, and he stands, lifting her to her feet. He puts his arms around her and stands holding her. She is so thin, and he thinks he might hurt her, but she doesn't cry out. He feels her warm breath in the hollow of his shoulder. Slowly, they part and with his arm around her, he picks up his soaked shorts and they climb through the fence and walk back to the camper. Inside, Tonio lights the lantern, picks up a towel, and begins to rub her hair. He dries her shoulders, her arms, and then, on his knees, wipes her hips and legs. When he finishes, he puts his cheek against her stomach and stays that way until he can feel her crying.

"God, Maia," he says, "I want to take care of you, be with you. It's all that matters." He looks up at her.

She puts her face in her hands for a moment and wipes the tears away. She smiles down at him. "It's not all that matters. This work matters, this search and recovery we are here to do. What just happened here is very beautiful, but it is also very, very complicated." She smooths his hair back. "Now I am suddenly cold." She goes over to her bag and crawls in. "Please get some sleep, my lovely boy."

Tonio dries himself and then kneels and kisses Maia on the lips, a deep, warm kiss that tells him that things have changed between them. He wants to say I love you, but he says instead, "I am here for you as long as you need me. Good night." He turns down the lantern and crawls into his bag. The rain beats down steadily outside. His mind races. He has found Maia and now seemingly may have lost her the same night. He understands that she is trying to keep him at a distance, and yet what she said about wanting him was real, too. Their being here together, after love-making, suddenly brings his life back into sharp focus. This experience, he suddenly knows, is not his experience or her experience, but a him/her fusion experience, one without a certain ending. This was to be their story now.

In the morning, with two amphoras containing mysteries, they arrive in Selcuk to return the ironing board to Filiz and, of course, to share their find. Filiz is waiting and laughs to see the board on the roof of the camper.

"You children amaze me, but also make me feel old."

"But not useless my dear one," Maia says. "Without your board all might have been lost, including Tonio. It supported the ancient tomb and brought us treasure."

"May I see?" she whispers. "But come in, come in."

Tonio sets his pack on the dining room table, opens it, and brings out the two amphoras. Filiz touches both and closes her eyes in prayer, her lips moving silently. Tonio turns one on its side and tells Filiz to lean close as he rolls it slightly. There is a sliding sound, then a small thump, then sliding and another thump.

Filiz has tears in her eyes. "It is, Maia, as your mother said. I hope Gregorios will tell us what it contains."

"Tonio thinks it is a list of church accounts," Maia whispers.

Filiz hits Tonio's arm. "That's terrible, you naughty boy," she says laughing. "But thank you for letting me touch them. I know they can't be opened, and you must avoid bumps in the road, and such."

Maia says, "Almost all of the next days will be on the water, and then they will be in Gregorios' careful hands."

"Bless you both, Blessings to God and Magdalene." She doesn't cross herself but kisses her thumb. "Can I get you coffee or some nice tea?"

"We have to go through customs and get on the Samos ferry to make connections to Crete. But thank you, dear."

Tonio says, "I would like to use the bathroom, please."

"Of course, Filiz replies, and watches Tonio leave the room. "Oh Maia, what a treasure you have found in that one."

"I know, Filiz. What happens now I have no idea. Oh, I must caution you. If you call Mother, be careful what you say, perhaps just that the visit was successful. She will understand.

"I can say too that Tonio is such a nice young man, and so resourceful."

"That too."

On the road again, relieved of the ironing board, they watch the road and talk of small details and how they will meet the challenge of the customs officers.

Tonio asks, "Won't they be searching for drugs?"

Maia says, "People, especially young ones, usually smuggle drugs into Turkey not out."

"Seriously, though . . ."

Maia touches his arm. "We will think of something. We just have to smile and be happy."

Waiting on the quay for the ferry to empty out from its third and final run for the day, they are quiet. Finally Maia says, "It's Friday afternoon, the weekend is here. Perhaps they will hurry us through." She gives Tonio his ring. "We can be in love and romantic."

"That won't be hard to play."

At the gate, after passports, with a guard looking into the back, the officer says, "Didn't you buy a rug? Nothing to take home?" There is a pause.

Maia suddenly holds up her finger and says, holding up Tonio's hand. "Oh yes, we bought these beautiful rings, for a better price than we could get in Athens. We were so lucky."

The official smiles and waves them on.

Tonio lets out a whistling breath. "That was brilliant. I would not have thought of it."

"I am not even sure it's true about prices, but I thought that in a place like Selcuk or even Kusadasi, gold might be cheaper than in Athens. But I also felt that we were protected at that moment."

"Perhaps it was your mother speaking."

"Remember it was she who told me to buy the rings in the first place."

"I cannot wait to meet this woman."

As they drive on to the quay in Lesbos, Maia points to a building. "There, do you see the sign for the Post? Park over there and I will go in and ask about boat schedules."

While he waits, Tonio, for the first time, has a moment to reflect on the last forty-eight hours and to imagine what might come next. It was such an overwhelming week, not even a week really, and yet everything has changed, perhaps even his entire life. What have they done? If there is value in the amphoras, the whole world will want to know where they were found. Turkey will demand return, and they might even be arrested. Could they make up a story about how and where they were found? Perhaps this Gregorios or Maia's mother will have an idea. And Maia. What will happen? Will he lose her? Will she even want to be with him? Marry. I've pretty much lost control of my life, he thinks. Maybe the idea of control is overrated. As he sits there quietly, he feels that something has changed in him. He looks up and watches Maia as she walks to the camper.

Maia opens the door and climbs in. "There is a small tanker headed for Naxos later today. It costs one hundred twenty Euros, expensive, but the boat goes on to Rodos, which is closer to Crete. There is frequent ship traffic out of Rodos."

Tonio pulls out his map of Greece. "Rodos is Rhodes, right?" She nods. On his phone he opens a map from Rhodes to Crete. "Four hundred kilometers, and they show a plane, too. But I don't expect we can risk a baggage search. If we're lucky, more dollars will get us there. I was thinking about how we must always stay with the camper. Someone might break in, looking for drugs, or money, or whatever, and this vehicle would not be hard to break into."

"Yes," Maia nods. "That is my thought too. I am even hesitant to call my mother to tell her about the find. Calls are not secure."

"Well, she probably knows everything anyway. Filiz might call her or, as you tell me, she will dream of everything."

"I told Filiz to call and we agreed what to say." She reaches over and smooths Tonio's furrowed brow. "As long as we are careful," she says, we shall be alright, I know it." Tonio takes her hand and kisses it.

Once in the dark hold of the tanker, where the camper will be safe, they go up on deck to watch the trucks and vans enter the hold. A small craft leaves the dock, headed out to a large white cruise ship. Leaning on the rail, Tonio watches as a few people wave. He waves back.

Maia laughs. "Do you wish you were with them, going out to drinks, a fine dinner, dancing and music, the life without troubles?"

"I've never been on such a ship, and I doubt I ever will be. Don't forget where you found me, sweating in a storeroom in the Agora. It wasn't my choice to be there at all, but just accepting the call was part of my life, finishing a long education, sweating a dissertation and, if I was lucky, finding a place to teach on a salary too low to buy a ticket to cruise the Mediterranean."

"Perhaps," Maia begins, "just perhaps your life will go in a different direction."

"Yes, I'm counting on it. I'm going to Crete, and that's unexpected enough for now."

GATE NUMBER
SIX

AFTER NEARLY two weeks of living out of the camper on the sea, Tonio and Maia said good-bye to a cleaned and nearly spotless vehicle and left it on the busy dock in Heraklion, the capital of the island of Crete. Now they sit on the sea wall, with Tonio's backpack at his feet, waiting for the car coming to pick them up.

Maia explains: "Santos is coming to get us. He is the son of Gregorios and Greta and takes care of shopping and my father's needs."

Tonio exclaims, "I thought Gregorios was a monk!"

"A liberated monk. He married Greta, who is Swiss, after their group disbanded. Greta takes care of the household and, with Mother, cooks for everyone."

"Is that everybody?"

"Yes. As I said, the house was once a small monastery of twenty or so monks. But as the Brotherhood aged, died, or went elsewhere, my parents bought the building and invited Gregorios to stay on. Father retired from shipping produce from the island to the rest of the Mediterranean and began a study of the Hermetic materials as a result of spending time in Egypt. He's in a wheelchair now after a stroke, but he's tough and fun to be around. The right side of his face droops a little and his right arm has limited use. He won't offer to shake hands or else he'll offer his left."

A car pulls up. "Here's Santos." A smiling young man with sandy hair and bright blue eyes runs over to them and gives Maia a hug and shakes Tonio's hand. "Welcome," in Greek and then another welcome in English. He reaches for the backpack, but Tonio says, "Thank you, I have it."

Santos steps back. Is that . . .?

"Yes," Maia says.

Santos raises his hands and backs up. "Wonderful. Father has been pacing and finding it hard to study, not knowing anything."

Maia says, "That makes all of us. We did not dare try to open what we have. Tonio thinks it may be only church records."

Santos says, "Oh no. But you are joking, yes?"

Getting into the back seat of the car, Tonio says, "Yes, of course, but it helps to keep us both calm and realistic."

The ride takes a little more than an hour, to Rethymno, a smaller city on the north coast. Maia explains that the city is a growing cultural center, quieter than Heraklion, and their house is in the hills above. "It even has a wall around it and very few houses nearby. The regulars in the cafe in town call it the Spiros Sanctuary."

The road up from Rethymno winds through fields and cypress trees to a long driveway and the walled compound with an imposing gate, open and welcoming. The sequence of greetings is for both new arrivals in the Great Room a whirlwind of kisses, hugs, exclamations, and questions until Tonio unpacks the amphoras and places them on a side table. Then a quiet descends. The white-haired and bearded Gregorios approaches and, as everyone watches, he first smells each amphora, then gently caresses the sides of each, then looks carefully at the sealed tops.

Tonio breaks the silence. "When we rolled them and listened, we heard a scratching sort of noise and then in one of them a thump as if something rolled over."

The old monk nods. "The neck is wide enough to insert a scroll. A wine jug has a narrower neck. These jars were made differently. The chances are good that scrolls are within, but of course success depends on their present condition. The climate in Selcuk is not like the desert, which keeps material dry, and we do not know what the material is yet. The worst luck would be that any writing will be so faded that we would need highly technical equipment, and that would mean including outside help."

Maia's father says, "And that, of course, would both be dangerous and take the contents out of our hands. With that in mind, we have rented a small climate-controlled vault for Gregorios' use. It has drawers and glass covers. If another is needed, we can get one."

Gregorios picks up a jar and holding it near his ear, says, "We are all anxious to know what these jars contain, but we will have to be very cautious. Santos and I will work in my study and you are welcome to watch us work. Much was learned years ago in working with the Dead Sea Scrolls and we shall avoid the same tragic errors. The Spirit in these jars will be with us." With that, Gregorios and Santos carry the jars out of the room and up the main staircase. Tonio is at once relieved and anxious to see them leave his sight.

Maia touches his arm. "They are in good hands."

"Yes, of course. I admire how Gregorios handles them. I must ask him about what he learned, if anything, from the smell. I imagine mostly exhaust and fuel oil, and the odor of my backpack."

Maia laughs. "Gregorios is like a bloodhound."

Standing beside her, Greta adds, "He can smell burnt toast three floors away."

"Speaking of which," Maia says, "can I help you with dinner?"

"Yes, come Maia," her mother says, "We three have a glorious dinner to prepare.

Alone with Mr. Spiros, Tonio follows the wheelchair from one side of the room to the other, from one bookshelf to another as Spiros explains his studies and how he discovered the Hermetica in Alexandria in the new library, which he refers to as "the spaceship."

"Tell me Mr. Spiros," Tonio begins . . .

"Vassili, please," Spiros says. "We do not stand upon formalities here. I like to think we are all the same age, in the middle of a journey from one stage to another. I think my soul was once a young student of Hypatia, the gifted teacher of Plotinus' vision, lecturing in the ancient library before it burned down, and I was unable to rescue her from the Christian mob that dragged her from her chariot in the square and skinned her alive. I will carry that memory to my future embodiments. It is a shame I carry."

Tonio says, "Yes, not the sort of thing taught in Sunday school. I read a fine biography of her in graduate school."

"What an unusual selection for graduate studies."

"Well," Tonio offers, "it was during a feminist period."

Vassili laughs. "I see. Search these shelves at your leisure, my boy. There is much here to catch your eye."

"I will. Thank you." Tonio scans the room. It seems there are a thousand books lining the walls.

Vassili says, "These are not all my purchases. Some were left by the monks, some in Latin. Do you . . .?

Tonio shakes his head. "Only in secondary school, long forgotten. For my graduate studies, I chose Greek, but I learned when I arrived in Greece that Classical Greek has only marginal use, not for ordering lunch for example."

Vassili nods. "But you read, no?"

"Oh, yes, fortunately, or else I couldn't do my work, which is to study the Mycenaean development of tholos tombs as a key to their cultural and spiritual beliefs."

"Yes, as Maia told us . . . and now, we may learn something about why these amphoras were placed in this tomb. Do you have any thoughts?"

"Well, I have thought a great deal about that question in the days getting here. The only sane answer for me at present is that whoever took the trouble to create a false wall to hide them wanted desperately to keep them away from someone and yet also just as desperately wanted them to be discovered someday, only perhaps not as long as it has been."

Vassili is silent, and then, "In spiritual matters, time does not exist. If there are scrolls that we have, they were written yesterday and tomorrow we will read them in the eternal Now."

After a rest and a guided tour of the herb garden with Gregorios, Maia and Tonio are summoned to dinner. The sun falls under the wall and the air cools from the late July heat. The dining room is filled with aromas. Vassili rolls to the head of the table and his wife Anna rules from the foot. Maia sits at her father's left and Tonio at Anna's right, with Gregorios across and Greta standing at the center chair ready to serve and Santos opposite. It will be the pattern for all their meals together.

"First," Anna begins, "this is our first meal of a new time with our accomplished new guest and the treasure that Maia and Tonio have brought with them from so far away, a place where our dear Magdalene lived out her days. For this new time and opportunity, we give thanks. So, now Greta will serve slices of sautéed haloumi cheese with Greek grappa and grapes. Our red wine this evening is a lovely bottle of a blend from the southern vines of Crete."

As those plates are cleared, there appears grilled wild sea scallops with white beans and arugula, served with a dressing of olive oil from the hills above Knossos. The main dish is marinated lamb chops, with stuffed eggplant. After dinner out comes a mild retsina to go with a delicate herb ice cream with dark chocolate, this in honor of Tonio, Anna explains, as a touch of America.

After dinner, Maia draws Tonio aside and says, "I'm tired Tonio. Will you walk with me upstairs?" They excuse themselves, and with his arm around her, they climb to the second floor and go down the long hall. Maia stops at a door. "Here's my room. Yours is there," pointing across the hall. Mother asked right out if we are 'intimate,' as she put it, and I said yes, but we agreed that we should have separate rooms. She leans in to him and they kiss. "I think you know already," she says, her hand on the doorknob, "that Father has much to share with you about his work."

Tonio smiles. "Yes, he has already begun. I shall be a faithful student."

Maia opens the door and finds the light switch. The room is long and narrow, with a simple cot bed, a small sink, desk and chair. "You see. We are privileged gluttons downstairs and humble seekers upstairs. Mother keeps a balance." She kisses his cheek and enters the room, closing the door. Tonio crosses the hall and opens the door to his room, which is the same. His pack is on the bed. He looks down the hall to the row of rooms, all seeming the same, and thinks he must ask where the bathroom is.

Back downstairs, Anna comes up to him and says, "Tonio, thank you for taking care of my precious daughter. She has told me that you love her and she you, I'm sure, but her illness puts a different color on our lives now."

"Of course. I know that my task was to help find what you sensed was there in Turkey but then, something else came to life. I'm not sure now what my role is, either here or in Maia's life."

Anna takes his hand and holds it for a minute without speaking. Then, "We hope you will stay, at least until we know what we have. You may be a help to Gregorios. He is getting old, and his experience is limited with this work, although he knows his early Greek, Coptic, and some Aramaic. Vassili and he have worked on the Coptic together now for several years."

"Well, my help will be limited to the Greek, but even then, I have a better grasp of the Classical period, which may not help. Biblical Greek, if that is what we have, is a different matter."

Then, from across the room, "Tonio, do you have a minute?"

Anna pats his hand and lets it go. "You have a good heart Tonio. Maia is right to have faith in you. Spend some time with Vassili. He craves a student." She smiles.

Tonio crosses the Great Room and when Vassili motions to a chair next to his desk, he sits.

Vassili begins, "I want to explain a little why I became a student of the Coptic Church. In business trips to Egypt, mostly to Alexandria, I was invited by clients to attend services in the Coptic churches. At first, I was put off by the elaborate robes and decorative interiors and by the incense filling the space, but then I learned that the Coptic Church is the oldest of the Christian churches, established, as the story goes, by the Apostle Mark as early as the first century. I became a student, then, because of Hypatia. I knew of course that what I saw twenty years ago now was not what a service was like in her time, and I knew as well that she declined the invitation and pressure to become a Christian. But I also knew it was not the same in Mark's time as it was in hers. So, I began to try and recreate that early Church." Vassili pauses and takes a sip of an espresso.

Tonio asks, "What did you find?"

"Yes, that was the question. First, I talked to my clients and then to the priests, but they knew little. I then went to the new library and found scholars who had opinions and a few historical details. But then I went to the Nag Hammadi materials and I found this saying of Jesus: "Do not lay down any rules beyond what I appointed you, and do not give law like the lawgiver lest you be constrained by it." I thought long on this, coming from Jesus through Mary, and I wondered much about what it meant. Then back here, I found the Brotherhood of the three Marys, here in this house, and they said they believed Jesus was warning against too many external rules or laws, and that meant to me a formal church with many doctrines. And more, it meant that the Early Fathers forgot or never learned about this warning." He pauses, finishes his espresso and says, "When Anna and her dreaming focused on this question, she had a clear image of the Cave of the Sleepers near Ephesus, where we knew that the Virgin and Magdalene, led by John, came and where they remained."

Tonio asks, "So you don't think Magdalene, after the death of the Virgin, left and went to France and lived out her life in a cave?"

"Anna doesn't think so, and I trust her intuitions. But if what you found offers a clue, we may know more of her final years. Gregorios may help us. I think he has held on to life waiting for this opportunity."

Tonio nods. "I wonder about what you said about Mark, but wasn't it John who guided the Marys to Ephesus? And if so, wouldn't he have been an influence on Magdalene?"

"Yes, but remember, if this John was the writer of Revelation, he was on Patmos, perhaps for a long time in meditation, and was more interested in the End Times and not so much about the Early Church. And remember there is as much confusion about the several Johns in scripture as there is about the Marys."

"I suppose, and if what you say is true about what Jesus had to say about laws, it may explain his burst of anger in the temple, scattering the money changers."

"Yes, my boy," giving Tonio's arm a few vigorous shakes. "Exactly, and no wonder that the Pharisees asked Pilate for the death sentence. Jesus was a serious threat to their power as well as their wealth. If he became a leader, what would he do to change the temple worship?"

Tonio says, "I begin to see now how this house and the whole mystery of the Marys in the gospels has captured your attention. It's not just a research project is it?"

Vassili backs his chair from the desk. "I'm glad you see it as well. You are a bright young man. I hope we will have time to explore together, but for now it is growing late, and you had a very long day. Do you know where your room is?"

"Yes, but I do have one question. Where is the bathroom among all the doors?"

Vassili laughs. "The last on the right. Either Anna or Greta would have supplied you with towels in your room, I assume. Sleep well, my boy, and we shall see what tomorrow brings. If I know Gregorios, he will have news in the morning."

The next morning, a bell sounds at seven o'clock. As people gather for breakfast, there appears at each place a bowl of muesli, rolled oats, fruit, and nuts in cream with a small Swiss flag stuck in the top.

Maia asks, "What is this?" whereupon Greta says, "Oh, Maia have you forgot? It is August first."

Tonio asks, "Which is . . .?' and Greta replies, "The Swiss anniversary of independence, over seven hundred years of freedom and peace."

"William Tell and the apple," Santos offers proudly. "How many nations can say that and at the same time remain neutral while the world burns?"

Gregorios enters the room. "So sorry to be tardy," and seeing the little flag at his place, looks at Greta. "So sorry my dear, but I have an excuse. Staying up late I opened one of the jars."

There is stillness and silence. Then, Anna . . . "And?"

"The contents are writing, on dark leather, in black and well-preserved. The scrolls were wrapped in animal skin, probably sheep or goat. The language is Greek. The strips are under glass in the vault. I will open the second after breakfast. Also, Vassili, we may need another vault."

"Just let me know. Such wonderful news my friend."

Then there is a pandemonium of hugs and exclamations and questions until Anna, sitting down, begins to eat her muesli and relative calm is restored.

Maia says, "But of course, Mother, you knew this all along."

Anna wags her finger. "Dreams are dreams. I have had many that never came to pass and others that turned out badly, or at least differently. But in this, I did have a feeling of certainty."

Gregorios eats his muesli with determination, and finishing, says, "I looked at one piece a little, from the beginning, and I think it is a letter, but not addressed to anyone or any place. My impression is that the writer, if Magdalene is the writer, was addressing someone around him or her." Looking around, he says, "I'm told we are blessed to have four people who have experience with ancient Greek. Tonio, are you one of the four?

"Yes, as Maia will tell you I am more at ease talking to Sophocles than in Greek to her."

Vassili says, "Good then, when Gregorios says that we can begin translation, we will set a schedule. Tonio, how long can you remain with us?"

"I am at your service. I will call my parents, who must be wondering where I am, but I'm free to be where I'm needed. Come fall, however, I will have to deal with my school obligations."

Gregorios rises, "I will invite you all to come to my work space when the second jar has been relieved of its treasure. Excuse me." Santos goes with him.

Anna rises as well. "Maia, perhaps we might take a walk before the day is too hot. I have some thoughts."

"Of course," and the two go outside, leaving Greta and Tonio to clear the dishes, while Vassili pours coffee and motors over to his desk.

In the kitchen, Greta washes and Tonio dries. "Tonio, I come from the German part of Switzerland, an area called the Appenzell in the town of Teufen. I was a nurse in a wonderful clinic called the Paracelsus Clinic of Alternative Medicine, named for the philosopher and healer who changed the way medicine is even now taught and applied. I met Gregorios when he was a patient, and we fell in love and married in the chapel there. I tell you this because I think Anna is now telling Maia that she should go there as soon as possible for treatment. To delay might be the end of her." Tonio puts down the dish in his hand and leans on the counter. Greta continues, putting a hand on his shoulder. "Anna has gifts and she spent time with Maia last night and helped her relax and get some sleep. She knows that Maia cannot continue to weaken her condition by taking such powerful drugs for pain. But she also knows that hope remains only if she acts soon and in the right way."

"By going to Switzerland."

"Yes, that is the plan. I am telling this to you because you are so close to her now. We will tell the others today. Gregorios has his work and Vassili and you can help."

"How does Vassili get upstairs?" Tonio asks.

"Ah," Greta says, "we have a small lift fitted to the outside, which stops at two floors where what were once windows are now doors. Now let us finish here, and you can join Vassili, but please say nothing until we know that Maia agrees."

"Yes, of course." Tonio pours himself some coffee. Cup in hand, he goes into the Great Room and takes his place, student to Professor Spiros, teacher of the Hermetica and seeker of mysteries.

When Maia and Anna return and Maia has gone to her room to rest, Anna explains the Swiss plan to Vassili and Tonio. What is additional news to Tonio is that it will be Greta who will travel and stay at the clinic, a fact which is also news to Greta.

"Maia made the suggestion about Greta," Anna explains, and of course it makes sense. Maia knows that Greta is familiar with the clinic and having her there will ease her anxieties, and I agree."

Tonio asks, "When will she leave?"

"Tomorrow. The clinic has a place for what could be a stay of a month or so and a plan for her treatment. I sent them the surgical report from the hospital in Paris, and then when I spoke by phone with them yesterday, they said that they feel positive about the plan they have for her. I think they have a protocol around immunology, using her own immune system to fight the disease. The clinic offers not only the immune system treatment but also a program of what they call alkaline/acid balancing. In the case of cancer, the professional experience of their doctors is that it has been successful in killing cancer cells. I'm sorry, Tonio, that we have been somewhat secretive about this, but I decided not to tell even Maia until we have an encouraging report from the clinic."

"But I know Maia wants to know what we have found. How can we get that information to her?"

"I know Tonio. We will find a way. But to delay now might mean we could lose her. I suggested to Maia that you both take a drive to the mountains this afternoon, only if you wish, of course."

And so, that afternoon, with a picnic lunch, Maia and Tonio drive up into the mountains. They park near a trail that leads into the woods and opens out to a field with a view to the sea. The drive was quiet, with little talk about the clinic.

Tonio explains about his conversation with Greta. "She didn't even know that she would be going with you rather than your mother."

"I told Mother that Greta would be more useful, knowing the place, and that I would be more confident with her there instead. I told her she would be just as useful at a distance, and that we'll talk on the phone. When she expressed concern about dealing with Father, I offered your help. Santos knows everything Father needs, and I can see he loves having you here. I hope you will stay for a while."

"This morning your father gave me a thin volume, The Way of Hermes, and said we could go through it together. And of course, there are the scrolls."

In the silence that follows, Maia takes Tonio's hand and holds it to her cheek. "Tonio. I know that soon you must think of going back to America. Have you thought about it?"

"Of course," he replies, "but only after working on the scrolls for a time. It's not easy to think about leaving."

"But it is necessary now. I'm sorry. I don't want to take you away from the scrolls." There is a pause.

"Do you love me, Maia?" He doesn't look at her.

"It is not a fair question now, Tonio. You know how I feel."

"I don't really. You said, once, the night of the rain, that you wanted my strength, that you felt I might give you the strength you need to get better. Do you remember that?"

"Yes," Maia says. "Of course, I remember."

"Was that it, then?" Tonio asks. "I mean, was that what drew you to me? Strength? The boundless energy of youth?" He couldn't keep the edge of sarcasm from sounding in his voice.

Maia looks down the hill. "Don't make this more difficult than it is, Tonio. I'm sure there is some truth to that, I mean being drawn to you in that way. We would have to get to know one another in a normal way, under different conditions. I am five years older, and it feels right now, the way I feel, more like ten." Tonio stands and walks a few steps away. "And I don't mean because it is you who is young. I know you don't care about that, but it is a fact. We come from different worlds. I know very little about yours. I don't think I could ever live in America, be a part of that culture. I am home now. This is who I am." With that she raises her arm and sweeps it toward the sea.

Tonio sees the gesture and feels in his chest the ache he has been carrying with him ever since he saw that arm sweep through the air for the first time. But now it is like a sword. He sits down on the grass as if sliced in two. The fight goes out of him. He says finally, "I know I have to go back and resolve all the things there. But I don't consider this relationship at an end."

Maia says, "I am not speaking of endings either. I don't know what tomorrow holds, or the next week or month. I cannot think about anything beyond that. Please understand. But don't speak about endings. After all, you have a real interest in the scrolls, and I would expect you to pursue that. Whatever happens to them involves you. It is just that right now . . . Mother said to me, it is important for me to put my mind on what the clinic has for me. As much as I care for you, it complicates my life now, and I need all the strength I have for what is to come."

Tonio is silent, then, "Would it be alright to call or send email?"

"Email will be best because I can reply when the time is right, when I am free to reply. Mother says I will sleep a good deal." She smiles. "Whatever happens, my Toni-oo, we have the rain and the grass and those moments when I felt your energy pour into me."

The drive back is quiet, and Maia needs to rest. Tonio walks her to her room and then returns to the Great Room. When he enters everyone is gathered at Vassili's desk, on which is a small box several inches square, wrapped in what looks like leather.

Seeing Tonio, Gregorios says, "I was just telling everyone that when I opened the second jar, which also contains scrolls, there was also this little package, and when I picked it up, I felt a sensation, like a slight vibration, and I felt warm and a sensation in my spine."

"A frisson," Anna said. "We have all felt it."

She picks up the package and gives it to Tonio, who reacts by quickly putting it down. "My God, what is this? I mean, I didn't feel anything when I handled the jar."

Gregorios said, "It could be exposure to the air."

Vassili says, "We should unwrap it and see what it is."

"It is why I brought it down to you," says Gregorios. "I did not dare to open it myself." He hands a small knife to Anna who carefully removes the wrapping, revealing a white stone box.

"It looks like alabaster," Anna says, moving a finger over its surface.

There is a cover, sealed. She inserts the blade and carefully cuts around the cover until it gives way. An aroma rises. Anna says, "It is eucalyptus."

In the box is another wrapped package, tied with a leather cord. Anna cuts the cord and slowly removes the thin skin wrapping. What emerges is a lock of hair. Gregorios steps back and kisses his thumb. "It is hers," he says. "Magdalene or even Mother Mary."

Anna picks up the lock. "It is her signature." She puts it back and replaces the cover. "We will keep this box wrapped and in the jar, sealed. It is the only evidence we have of something from the source. Surely these hairs can be dated."

Vassili adds, "And DNA can reveal heritage. If so, Mary's might even suggest the link to the people of Magdala."

Each person standing there has an explanation of this mystery, but they know enough to let their thoughts remain unspoken, at least until the scrolls might offer answers. In the meantime, much must be done to prepare for Maia's departure.

Anna goes with Gregorios to his workroom, carrying the box. Placing it on a table, she says, "Gregorios, I ask for your confidence and care in what I am to do. I want you to take one hair and I will put it in a locket which I will wrap carefully and place in Maia's suitcase. It will be a talisman and we will trust in its healing powers. Do you agree?"

"My Lady, even one hair if indeed it is from Mary, it will have healing powers."

"I agree. Carefully remove one hair. I will be right back," and she leaves. A few minutes later, she returns with a locket. Gregorios places the hair in the locket and snaps it closed. Anna kisses his cheek and goes down to help Maia pack.

The next day, Maia and Greta board a flight from Heraklion to Zurich. In the house there is something of a pall, but Anna keeps up the spirits of the remaining five by focusing attention on the task before them. Tonio helps Vassili into the lift and then takes the stairs three at time to arrive on the third floor before the lift does.

Vassili is impressed. "My word, young man, such speed, but do not race down the same way. You will break a leg."

They enter the workroom, greeted by the whir of an air conditioner and a dehumidifier. Gregorios is working on a strip of text, peering through a large magnifying glass attached to a mounted arm. The strip is under a sheet of glass, shielding the text from warm breath and dust. Looking up he points over at another table and says, "I have only one additional setup for examining a strip of text, so you will have to take turns. As yet, I am not sure of a proper order, but when I am, the work will move more quickly because we will have a context to help us with both words and meaning. I am sorry for the close quarters. This room is too small to be a real scriptorium but being small it is easier to keep cool and dry in the summer heat and humidity."

Vassili says, "Tonio, you start over there. I will stay with Gregorios for a time and watch." With that, he moves his chair to a position near the table but not really close enough to look at the text. Tonio sits at the next table, with Santos at his side, and draws the magnifier to the strip of text. He knows this is not fifth-century text, but he also knows that the tradition is that the Greeks renew their language every four hundred years, trying to maintain enough of the ancient forms for students to be able to read Homer in the original. Nevertheless, this will be a test for him.

As Tonio looks down through the strip of words, he recognizes the repetition of the word nous, or 'mind.' He says, "Excuse me, but I notice in this strip of text the repetition of nous, or mind. Do you see that?"

Gregorios replies, "Yes, I saw that in another strip too. I am reminded of Paul's first letter to the Corinthians, verse 2:16: 'For who has known the mind of the Lord, that he may instruct him? But we have the mind of Christ.' Perhaps reference to that verse appears here."

Tonio studies the text further and begins thinking about possible meanings for 'mind'. He knows from his own church days that the sentence, "We have the mind of Christ" traditionally meant "we have the gospels and the parables."

Santos asks, "What else can mind mean, if not the gospels?"

Tonio looks over at Gregorios, who is peering into his magnifier and making notes. Waiting until Gregorios straightens up to stretch, Tonio says, "I know the usual reading of having the mind of Christ, but I wonder if there's another deeper sense of it. We know from the Pre-Socratics that nous was thought of as something attuned to Logos, as central to the cosmos, that mind in Anaxagoras was the Greater Mind, and was universal. And in recent years, physics and cosmology are speaking of mind in a similar light, calling it universal consciousness. It is the idea that without such a consciousness the universe would not even exist. In that sense Paul could have meant that. After all, he had a serious personal crisis turned to insight on the road to Damascus, which could have been a glimpse of that universal nature of mind. What do you think?"

Gregorios stares at Tonio for a few moments and then says, "Please take notes on this."

Vassili has been silent, but now he says, "What Tonio said may be a key. After all, if all that is meant are the words of Jesus in the gospels, then Paul would have used the word logos, which means both 'word' and something larger like spirit or Being. But, as we learn in the Gospel of Mary, Jesus said mind specifically. Also, when this text was written, perhaps, the gospels had yet to appear, so that nous might well mean what Tonio describes."

They work through the afternoon, happy to finally be working with what they had hoped would be their task. Sitting later around the table after a light supper, Tonio brings up the subject of mind again, explaining it to Anna and adding the notion that in the Renaissance the discovery of the Hermetic materials also introduced the notion of a universal mind.

Vassili turns his chair and goes over to the books, saying as he goes, "Yes, yes, I have a translation from Ficino who wrote on this subject." And so the discussion goes into the evening, with nous as the focus of a new understanding.

Later in his room, Tonio finds an email from Maia on his phone. She and Greta arrived in Zurich and took the train to St. Gallen, and then south to the clinic, which is beautiful, and people are kind and encouraging. Greta found no one from her past but was accepted warmly and is already helping in the clinic. Maia sends her love to him and to everyone. Last, she says that the locket her mother gave her is pressed warmly on her chest and yes, she promises not to open it, but why she doesn't know (question and exclamation mark). Tonio replies to talk about his idea about mind. He doesn't mention the locket mystery.

Four days later, while work continues in what Vassili insists be called the Spiros Scriptorium, Gregorios reads his notes from a strip of text. "The writer says, 'It is wise, before reading these words, to recite the word Maranatha in praise and supplication.'"

"What is maranatha?" Tonio asks.

"It means roughly 'Come Lord!' Or 'Oh, Lord, Come!' An invocation. Or a mantra to be repeated."

"Go on."

"The scroll is an account of a life. It begins with a greeting to believers, followers. Christians or Jews, for the moment. Then the writer says that he or she is making or giving an account of Magdalini, Our earthly Mother and First Apostle." He pauses. "What do you think?"

Tonio says, "Well, that suggests clearly that the letter or account is about but not by Magdalene."

Vassili interjects, "What you have may be an introduction. Perhaps the next or one after will be in her hand."

"Or dictation," Tonio offers.

As another week of intense work passes. It becomes clear that Gregorios does indeed have what he termed a testimonial for Mary Magdalene and which also paid respects to the passing of Mother Mary, who was buried near her little house in Ephesus, high above and looking down on the great Temple of Artemis, the ancient Earth Mother of earlier times. What remains now of that tradition is the presence of a simple stone house near a spring, where women go to pray and bring food to the two nuns who keep candles lit and accept donations from the faithful who visit. The Roman Church has finally accepted the tradition that the Holy Mother did indeed live out her life in Ephesus but still holds to the tradition that she ascended bodily to Heaven.

In that week Gregorios completed one scroll and he and Vassili worked on an English translation, which after supper one evening Gregorios read from his notes. A picture has begun to emerge of a young man who was doing the writing. He was a follower of John and was also in service to Mary. The memoir was evidently written as a request either from Mary or others who asked him to urge Mary to speak. References to Mary's reluctance to speak are frequent. It was, Gregorios thought, both true and a device, an affirmation of great humility on Mary's part, as if she did not wish to place herself above those she served. There are references, for example, to past conflicts with Peter over the role of women in the teaching. And yet, there is also in the text a striking confidence as well. At one point, in a clear passage, the writer speaks of Mary as "knowing the mind of Rabbani, or 'Master' and 'being at one with his mind in all things.'"

Vassili wonders, "What did she mean by being at one with his mind?" Answering his own question, he says, "It could be as simple as agreeing with the Master, but I think we are seeing something much deeper. She was a part of his mind, within it. In the Hermetic tradition, the teacher and student access the same mind, the nous of the early Greeks such as Anaxagoras, whom Tonio mentioned and who was known in Athens as Mind. He argued that the key to the truth is to live within the greater mind of the cosmos. We have the phrase, 'being of one mind,' but it means so much more than mere agreement. Anaxagoras taught that it is nous that actually creates and sustains the cosmos."

Tonio nods. "The same for Heraclitus a little earlier, five hundred years before Christ. He said the cosmos was ruled by the Logos, which means Spirit or simply the One. Later Logos and Mind were discussed and debated together. How was that brilliance lost? The sad truth is that later—after Jesus was crucified and his followers, especially Paul, wandered the Mediterranean and established communities of believers, which in itself was all well and good—within two or three centuries, the so-called Early Church Fathers abandoned Greek philosophy and created instead an elaborate mythology that believers were encouraged or required understand and accept."

"Indeed," Vassili adds. "The sad fact is that the actual truth was too abstract for ordinary people to grasp. It was the newly crowned Bishops who set aside esoteric teaching in favor of preaching a simplified message."

Anna adds, "Sad to say that so much time has passed and yet the attitudes that Mary fought so hard to change still rule among the Christian sects, East and West. So few women have influence or power, even now. Men find a tradition of power for themselves within the religion, even as it passes away in the culture. It is no wonder that in so many countries fewer and fewer attend church and yet nothing changes or changes only in small, insignificant ways. I once argued with Maia about this, but now, from this past, we discover a woman of such power, I cannot help but agree with her."

Tonio asks, "What would you do? I mean, it seems to me that religions come and go, but the Bible-based religions seem destined to go on forever in one form or another, like the change from Latin to English."

"And yet, what is strange," Anna replies, "is that the 'Biblical religions' as you call them, are based on the same God and even the same prophets, except for Muhammad, of course. I envision a future when all religions fade away by default and are replaced by a spiritual reality with no leader or rules or laws."

"How could that happen?" Tonio asks.

"In the Gospel of Mary," Vassili says, "from the Coptic sources, Jesus tells Mary that 'there is no sin' and I believe he meant that any religion that claims an Original Sin is preaching an evil and that it is destructive to condemn humanity as essentially evil in its nature."

Tonio asks, "Then how did the idea of Original Sin come to be doctrine?"

Vassili explains, "Remember, Tonio, that piece of teaching from Jesus was lost and in the case of the Nag Hammadi gospel came to light only in 1945. Original Sin was formulated by Saint Augustine in the fourth century to claim that Jesus died to save collective humanity from the sin of disobedience in the Garden. But in the gospel, Jesus tells Mary that sin comes from personal action, individual disobedience like adultery or murder. You could say, although we sin, we are not fundamentally sinners."

Gregorios nods. "We hope, Tonio, that when Anna had her dream about the scrolls and how the place of them came to her after the earthquake were signs of all our hopes for the world. Mary may say something in these scrolls about similar hopes and that the Lord spoke clearly about it."

Vassili says, "We see in the Coptic gospel that Jesus told Mary that there should be no laws made from his death, but rather to go forth and speak the truth about his way of life and his victory over death. If he truly died for us, it was only that we should know that we shall never die, that we must know our souls as the true nature of our being. Our concern is based on how the Bible, both old and new, has been misused by the absolutists who claim truth in every word or poorly translated word, and by those who preach for reasons not even framed in the content, claiming worldly riches for believers, when it is the gifts of the spirit which are its core message. I think of both the old and new testaments as descriptions of the journey of the soul."

Anna stands. "But the body also has a journey, and it requires energy. I shall prepare something."

"Let me help," Tonio offers, also getting up.

It becomes a part of the routine that Tonio helps Anna with meals, or lunch and supper at least. On one occasion, as they were putting dishes away, Tonio asked about Anna's dreams, asking when she became aware of their significance. "I still don't understand," he said, "how you knew about Mary's letters and where they were."

Anna corrected him. "First, I did not know about the letters as such, even though we had been talking about the letters we have had now for some time, but I will tell you how this began."

An aroma permeated the kitchen. Anna said, "Let's sit for a minute. Espresso?"

"Thank you."

Taking a sip, Anna began. "This house was a sanctuary for displaced monks from Athos, what we call the Greek version of the Vatican. In one of the many monasteries, where every monk had a task, work that is done to provide for food, repair, copying scrolls, that sort of thing—there were several monks whose task it was to forage for root vegetables and mushrooms. One time, a serving of mushrooms caused a crisis when a half-dozen monks began having what appeared to be convulsions, but in fact were visions and hallucinations."

"Psilocybin," Tonio said.

"Yes. And there was an inquiry, tracing the event to the mushrooms. Well, the monks were blameless, but from that point on, the mushrooms were tested before each serving. What then happened, when a few of the monks began speaking of their experience, especially about visions of Jesus and angels and other iconic imagery, two monks decided to have similar experiences. It was not long before they identified the right mushrooms and secretly began to use them, usually taking their mushroom tea out in the woods where they would not be observed.

"And surely as night follows day, word spread."

Anna took a sip of coffee. "Indeed, and after a second investigation, four monks were banished from the monastery and from Mount Athos altogether. After searching for a safe place to serve, they arrived here, to what was an abandoned house, which they set about bringing back to life. Soon enough, as word traveled about the reason for their expulsion from Athos, others came and were curious."

"I assume," Tonio interjected, "that you are suggesting that this account has a bearing on your dreams?"

"Well, that part of the story takes much longer to tell, but yes. After a time, the monks gathered here experimented and, as a result, some left. There were conflicts, and the Monastery of the Three Marys was dissolved."

"Except for Gregorios."

"And two others, two of whom have died. Gregorios put the house up for sale, and we purchased it more than a decade ago. Now to the point. Gregorios shared the history of Athos and the experiences the monks shared. He also shared the books from people like Wasson and Hoffman and especially Stamets, documenting the history of psilocybin. In particular, and here I can answer your initial question, in Wasson's notes from his experiments in Mexico, reference is made to prophetic images. He said that he was worried about his son back in New York and while under the influence of mushroom tea, he saw his son and saw a crisis and its resolution, and when he returned to New York, his son related the same information."

"Did others have similar experiences?"

"Oh yes. Not always of course, but for me, I have found instances of great importance where a dream has proved to be true, the most important example being the dream that revealed Maia's illness."

"And the tomb? That too?"

"That too, but not in detail. What I have told no one, however, is that in my dream, following the earthquake, there was a glow in the tomb, not like a candle, but just a glow in the one area."

"I didn't see any glow, but I did feel a lightness in the anteroom, a different feeling from the rest of the tomb."

Anna nods. "That of course makes sense. In a dream a feeling would be visual to a sleeper."

"For me," Tonio replies, "I felt a lightness, and then my knowledge of tomb structure took over and I found the false wall."

Anna nodded. "It seems that these visions in dreams were

common and have been for centuries. We know, for example that the Eleusinian Mysteries employed an entheogen made from argot, which is a mold that forms on rye to enhance the ultimate moment of revelation as Persephone returns from the underworld. If you look through Vassili's books you will find ample references, that is, everything except the true visions of dreams. That source comes only from Wasson, as far as I know. But you might find others."

Back now to the present evening, Tonio approaches the subject of drugs and visions again. "The other evening, you told me the story of the monks and mushrooms, and . . ."

"You want to know if we have any mushrooms here now. Yes?"

"Well, yes."

"Tonio, first, let me talk to Vassili about this while you do some reading in the references I mentioned. I see no reason why you should not have this experience, but it is a major step in your development."

"I understand. Thank you. I will say that in graduate school, I did have an experience or two with LSD, but never psilocybin. However, I cannot imagine a safer place than right here to learn and study"

Anna rises and gives Tonio a hug. "That is true. Let us see what takes place."

"Have you had another dream about Maia?" Tonio asks.

"Only about her illness, but as yet nothing about what is to happen." Anna puts a hand on Tonio's arm. "I think that means that what is to happen depends on events that are unclear or unresolved. But that is why keeping a positive vision of her well-being is so important."

"Do you see anything of my journey?"

Anna smiles, "No, nothing yet."

"It's just that I don't know what I'm to do now."

Anna pats his arm. "There, you see, your future is as yet unformed. I have nothing to dream about."

Tonio smiles, "You spoke a while ago about the soul and its knowing. Can you say more?"

"The soul is a part of the human being, just like the brain which controls discursive thought. But the soul is independent and if it is ignored it tends to sleep, in a sense, not taking part in a person's life. But those who acknowledge the presence of the soul awaken it and it then participates in the life. What is necessary is to engage its activity and that happens in the body's energy system, the essential part of which is the spine. You know about the chakras, don't you?"

Tonio nods. "In Eastern meditation, the chakras are arranged through the body from the base of the spine to the top of the head, right?"

"Yes, but as to the soul, that movement tells us the level at which the soul is active. In Hermetica, we learn of the gates of the soul, which in the body are seven, and above that in terms of enlightenment and knowledge of the divine, go all the way to ten levels, or gates. In the Nag Hammadi there is a discourse on the eighth and ninth gates. In that account a young man who has reached the seventh gate, as high as a normal mortal can reach, asks to be elevated to the next two levels, which take him to the level where the Great Soul or Spirit resides. Such an elevation is the goal of all spiritual seekers while in the body."

Tonio asks, "Are you at the eighth or ninth level?"

"I do not know. I have no one to tell me. My dreams may or may not be part of that system, but I share this much with you so that you too may learn the way of the soul and learn to have its gifts as part of your life. It is where Maia lives today."

"Well," Tonio says, "I feel that in her and perhaps it is one reason I love her so."

"Be patient, Tonio. We shall see if her body wishes to keep its hold on her life."

Tonio enters the Great Room and finds the Nag Hammadi Library. Forgotten for a time were Mary's letters as he began a reading of the "Discourse of the Eighth and Ninth." That evening, he receives an email from Maia.

Subject: Report

I am thinking of you this evening
and wondering how your work
is coming along. Things here are
routine, with diet, mild exercise like
swimming, which I enjoy in the warm
waters that come from a natural spring.
We had a conference this morning and
the doctor said that I should plan on
another month, meaning September.
They have told me that I am a good
candidate for a CRISPR injection,
which evidently finds a flaw in my
DNA and may correct what caused
my illness. It is expensive but the
Swiss system is supporting.
Tonio, I urge you to take
this time to go home. You
know that Gregorios and Father will
be working for quite a long time.
This is a chance for you
to see to your studies and to find
out what you want to do. I care about
you very much. Love, M

As he lies in bed that evening, it becomes clear that Maia doesn't know what her prognosis is and doesn't want him to wait for news of her one way or another. Her comment that she cares about him was a carefully worded uncertainty. Whether she truly cares for him, loves him, is secondary he knows, and he determines that tomorrow he will announce his departure for America.

Before Tonio can leave the next morning, Vassili hands him a copy of the Nag Hammadi text and says, "I know the discourse is a short piece to read, but the right way to read it is that when you finish, go right back and start from the beginning and read as if you were continuing to read new material and not going back. Do that for about ten times, reading slower and slower. You will find that when you do that, each word will begin to vibrate in your mind and what lies behind the words will suddenly appear. That's the best way, and if that works for you, send a note and I will tell you how to read another discourse."

A little later the many heartfelt good-byes are supplemented by a packed lunch and numerous invitations to return at any time. Santos drives him to the airport and the Olympic Airways fifty-six-passenger jet to Athens. Before boarding, Tonio writes to Maia announcing his departure and then an email to Judith Diels, asking if she could have some time for him this afternoon, since his flight to Philadelphia isn't leaving until noon tomorrow.

The flight lands in Athens just as he finishes the lunch of select cheeses, some yogurt, and a banana. In a taxi, an email appears from Judith inviting him later that afternoon to her home, saying, "that way you won't run into the boss."

Sitting in her lush garden with lemonade and cake, Tonio tells Judith much of what has taken place, short of Maia's presence in a Swiss clinic and the discussion with Anna about dreams. As to how the scrolls were discovered, he puts the find in the Seven Sleepers Cave.

"The thing is," he concludes, "I'm concerned about the whole matter of taking the scrolls out of Turkey, especially if and when we want ever to publish them, which I imagine will be an option at some point."

Judith says, "Yes, I see your problem. As one who is neutral in the conflict between Turkey and Greece, I certainly agree that at some point those who are concerned with such things will want to trace the scrolls to their source. Not only will the countries be involved, but also the Orthodox officials and Rome will be even more thorough. Authenticity and provenance are exacting processes as well as principles."

"I'm in a difficult position because we, Maia and I, are the ones who actually committed what is certainly a theft of Turkish property. But we did so because her parents, who now possess the scrolls, don't want an official Church or any government to control them because what they contain may challenge the very structure of Church doctrines."

"I see. Well then, in this world, there are always various anti-religious groups and organizations that would love to have them, but your people don't seem to be the sort who would go in that direction."

"No."

"You said that these people live in a former monastery called the Brotherhood of the Three Marys. Is it possible that, say, in a renovation of the building, workers might have uncovered the scrolls, as if they had been hidden there for some time, perhaps years?"

"That's a great idea," Tonio says, sitting up a little straighter.

"Devious of course, and there would be a careful examination of the building and a great deal of inquiry. And oh, I must warn you, never, under any circumstances exchange phone or email or even letters about such a plan or one that even mentions scrolls. In fact, it's probably best if your friends thought of the idea themselves, as they just might."

Immediately, Tonio remembers Maia's email mentioning work rather than scrolls. Is Judith right about the danger? Is it even a danger after all?

Tonio says, "Thanks, Judith. We'll be careful. This is all rather new to me, so far is it from working on a dissertation."

"And what about that? Will you be able to pick up where you left off?"

"Good question. I don't really know. It may be hard to explain, but in the past two months my life has changed so much that my research never even came to mind, and that can't be good. Dissertations need to be in the forefront, not stored away, and I feel I've lost the thread."

"Give it some time, but don't let it go—that is, if your advisor is still willing to be there for you."

"Yes, there is that too. Professor Burnside hasn't contacted me, which of course may just mean he hasn't heard from Templeton. Has he said anything to you?"

"No. I don't think he knows that you and I share thoughts and ideas. He would be surprised to know that you're sitting in my garden right now."

"A good thing," Tonio says, smiling. He stands. "I have to be going. Thank you, Judith. I'll keep in touch, but not about 'you know what'."

They walk together to the gate. Judith pulls him down to give him a kiss on the cheek. "I like your beard," she says and waves as he goes out to the street.

In his hotel room near the airport, Tonio takes a long shower and slips into bed with the Nag Hammadi. Following Vassili's instructions, he reads the discourse, and reads again and then again, until both eyes and mind resist. The last thing he reads is, "Indeed the understanding dwells in you; in me it is as though the power were pregnant . . ." In his dream that follows, a naked

Maia is swimming in a pool and smiling up at him as he watches her. Greta stands by the pool holding a robe and Maia steps out of the water and slowly slips into the robe. She waves to Tonio and they walk away, but not before Greta turns and slowly waves. The pool is outdoors, and they walk into a field and toward the sun, which blinds Tonio as he tries to watch them.

In the morning, awakened by the scheduled call, he remembers the dream in detail, which is unusual for him. He wonders if his reading of the discourse last night had caused the dream and brings it to mind now. He had been thinking about what Anna said about past and future in dreams, the idea that the soul is timeless in its journey through embodiments. He has always thought that if we have a soul it would be personal, and if it isn't what is our relation to it? He must explore further.

Later, on the plane, he takes out the book and reads and rereads the discourse. When he comes again to the passage that reads, "My father, the progress that has come to me now and the foreknowledge, according to the books, that has come to me, exceeding the deficiency . . . these things are foremost in me . . ." he pauses and looks out the window at the clouds below, and thinks again of his dream. Was it foreknowledge? Why did she walk away and why did Greta smile and wave to him? The discourse tells us to pray with our mind, heart, and soul and that only then will the eighth gate open. But what is the eighth and what does it reveal? And how do we bring mind, heart, and soul together into a unity as Vassili said? What is that like? It comes to him then that Vassili's reading instructions might be a clue to finding this unity of perception. Part of his reading is intellectual and then sometimes it is his passion for the youth's desire to know, but what of the soul? What is that like? It isn't thought or feeling, although feeling at some level must be involved. Can we communicate with the soul? He wonders.

The plane follows the sun west, across the Atlantic, arriving in Philadelphia at four in the afternoon. He takes the train out to Haverford and a cab to his parents' house, a modern Colonial reproduction on a quiet street. His reception is mixed, happy to see him but also critical of his silence. Professor Fletcher sums up, "You know, son, how your mother worries."

At dinner in the formal dining room, Tonio explains as much as he dares about his long silence. He decides not to mention Crete or Maia at all, but to say that his research had taken him to Samos (which was somewhat true) in search of evidence of tholos tombs that far from any previously known Mycenaean activity. That settled, his mother comments on his beard ("makes you look older, not to mention making me feel old") and his father speaks about his appointment to the English Chair at the college.

"The administration is anxious about the decline of English majors and has put pressure on us to, as they phrased it, jazz up the program. Unfortunately, none of the younger instructors has tenure, so it has fallen to me. I may need you, Tonio, to give me a sense of what young people are reading these days."

Tonio laughs. "You want suggestions from someone who has his brain in Pre-archaic Greek history?"

"True, but you must read other things, if only to be able to talk to other young people."

Tonio thinks about the Eighth and Ninth discourse. "Well," he says, "now that I'm home, I'll keep your problem in mind, but you might send a questionnaire to last term's students and ask them what they're reading this summer."

"Goodness, that's a good idea! Will they be forthcoming, do you think?"

Tonio shrugs. "I have no idea. The current undergraduate scene seems years ago to me now. If they can get their noses out of their phones, maybe they still read. I don't envy your task."

Tonio's room is as he left it: a Haverford banner on the wall, a framed picture of himself being kissed by a dolphin while on spring break in Cancun, and an old Chromebook on his desk. He plugs it in and then opens his closet, where a wardrobe is hung neatly. He unpacks and puts the Nag Hammadi on his nightstand. Home, he thinks, looking around. Where is home and what do I do now?

Next day after breakfast, Tonio places a call to Dr. Burnside's office and is told by the department secretary that the chairman is surveying a dig in Guatemala but will return in two weeks. When asked if he wishes to leave a message, he declines.

Later that morning a beep on his phone signals an audio message. It's from Vassili. "Tonio, I trust you made it home safely and that perhaps you have been reading the discourse. Knowing you are in Pennsylvania, I took the opportunity to look up the addresses of Egyptian Coptic churches in that state. There are nine. I wrote to a few and one priest replied right away to say that he would be willing to meet with you. I said that you are interested in the Hermetic meaning of the Eighth and Ninth Gates. He understood right away. His church is in Allentown. His name is Father Awasi and here is his number: 848-555-7124. Everyone sends greetings, and Anna wants you to know that the renovation work in the cellar goes well. Blessings, Vassili.

Tonio is stunned. Anna must have thought of Judith's idea, or maybe dreamed it. He must find a way to ask. Mentioning Anna by name had to mean it was her idea. And if they had already begun work, they must be making further plans, perhaps even to announce the "discovery" of the scrolls. He calls the church in Allentown and is surprised that he can be received that afternoon. He replies to Vassili with news and thanks.

Borrowing his mother's aging Volvo, with a farcical story about visiting a professor of classics who is editing a book on a new theory about Mycenaean origins, he drives the sixty miles to Allentown and finds the church—which turns out to be a modern-looking structure with a contrasting gold Coptic cross on its steeple.

Father Awasi greets him at the door in his white and gold surplice. "I am happy to meet someone so interested in the Eighth and Ninth discourses, interested enough to come so far to inquire. Please, come in and we will sit in my office. I see you brought your text."

"Yes," Tonio replies, "and thank you for seeing me so quickly."

"Ah, well, when I hear of someone who wishes to know, to understand matters of the soul and spirit, I not only have an interest, but also a duty."

Awasi is a short man of middle age, of dark complexion, and is clearly Egyptian. Tonio is struck with the contrast between the plain exterior of the church compared to the ornate interior, the walls decorated with icons of Jesus, Mary, and the Apostles.

In his office, Father Awasi points to a chair as he sits behind his desk. "Well, I understand you are a graduate student and you are studying Hermetic themes, so your friend told me."

Tonio places the Nag Hammadi on the desk. "Yes, I'm working with Hermetic texts, but I want to learn from one who has the proper background and understanding, not so much about the history, but rather about the actual process that one follows."

"The process of what and to what end?"

"I mean in particular in the discourse of knowing the soul and using means to find the unity described in the text when the mind, heart, and soul become one."

"Good. What is your sense of the soul?"

Tonio pauses. "I don't think I have a sense of it, as you say."

Father Awasi looks out the window for a moment and then

says, "What kind of time do you have to devote for this search?"

"It seems to me that what I seek to learn should not have a time limit. Are you suggesting that perhaps we could meet from time to time?"

"Yes, I may be suggesting that. The truth is that when someone comes as you have and asks to acquire understanding of the soul as you have spoken of it, one who has knowledge to share on the subject cannot send the seeker away. Since the phone may ring, perhaps we could go outside to the patio, where there is shade and where nature can help also with the teaching."

They exit a side door and follow a path to a gate to a patio. Seated on metal chairs under a chestnut tree, Father Awasi tells Tonio to take off his shoes and socks, sit up straight, close his eyes and feel every place where his body meets the chair and where his feet meet the warmth of the patio stones. Then he tells him to open his ears and hear everything in his surroundings until his mind is still. Then, after a pause, the priest begins to speak of the soul, its place in the human system and relation to the mind and the heart. He explains that the soul needs to be addressed consciously and acknowledged consciously . . . and that Tonio must urge his soul to speak, but not as one would speak to another, but to listen for some sensory response to his request.

Here the priest pauses. Does he feel any physical reaction? If not, one must wait, but trust that the soul will communicate, not in the mind or at the level of feeling like a warmth, but as a physical presence in the body. Father Awasi presses Tonio for reactions. Tonio is uncertain and hesitant, trying to come to terms with something unexpected. Awasi gives him several exercises to practice, ways to give close attention to what signals the body is sending.

"What you must do is find time and space to practice this attention, attending not to thoughts, which occupy us nearly all the time, but rather to watch and listen to what the body and the soul may be saying to you. And next time you can report what you have learned from the body's communication. When your mind is still, and your emotions are quiet, the soul will be heard . . . and when that happens for you, our progress will begin."

Tonio asks a few questions about dreams, and Awasi says that there is much to learn there as well, but not for now. "First," he says, "give your attention to what the body is doing, watching and learning to listen to the soul, which wants to communicate here and now to a person who is awake. We must learn first what it means to be truly conscious, to generously give our attention to what is taking place within. Remember, if you wish to find a unity between body, mind, and soul, you must attend to these faculties, to understand the differences and resemblances. And remember this: In matters of unity, identity is the vanishing point of resemblance."

"Of resemblance?"

"Yes. By resemblance I mean knowing the difference between the qualities of mind, body, and soul and then finding how those differences fade away to an identity. We say in such moments that the body, mind, and soul are one. The soul announces its presence through the body and the mind recognizes, each having its proper function."

On the drive back to Haverford, Tonio reflects on the afternoon and what he's going to tell his parents about a series of visits to Allentown to speak to his imaginary Classics professor. He'll say that the professor has all these notes and maps that aren't in his own book and he needs to make sense of it all. The idea that he would tell them about Father Awasi is out of the question. His traditional Episcopal parents would never understand and would assume he has gone over to the freak side of culture. He remembers how his father reacted to Salinger's Franny and Zooey, especially when Franny hid in a bathroom reciting the

Jesus prayer over and over. Perhaps Salinger was writing about the vanishing point of resemblance in a toilet stall.

In the next weeks, after his meetings with Father Awasi, Tonio writes emails to Maia, trying not to press her with questions about her treatment or condition. It remains unspoken between them. But he tells her a little about his trips to Allentown and talks with Father Awasi and keeps it in line with his talks with Vassili on the Hermetica. He says that he has not yet had a conference with his dissertation advisor and that he is losing interest in tholos tombs, wondering how he can write without sounding bored. After all, a dissertation should be a passionate culmination of one's work over years of study. After several deleted drafts, he avoids any reference to hoping to see her soon or mentioning how much he misses her. It would only create stress, which is something she doesn't need.

At his next visit to see Father Awasi, Tonio decides to share his concern for Maia, not for advice exactly but more in response to the priest's sensitivity, his willingness to listen and provide caring words, which at one point he overheard when a phone call came as they were about to begin a session. As Tonio speaks about Maia's treatment in Switzerland, one comment meets his mood. Awasi says, "When you take responsibility for another's life, as you clearly have done, it awakens the soul and you become whole."

Tonio is stunned. "You mean that my soul has been asleep up to this point in my life?"

The priest smiles. "Well, 'sleep' is a term to suggest that perhaps in your life to this point, your primary concerns have been with self, or another way of speaking is that what we call your ego has been the master of your life rather than a servant. But when your soul truly awakens, the ego is diminished in its influence and returns to its proper function."

"Which is what?" Tonio asks.

"What we call the ego is really a fiction, but we can say that self-concern, as we might call it, cares for our own well-being in general. But now, in addition to your basic needs, your attention is focused on another being in a loving way. And it is the case that the soul becomes the master in your life, taking on the role once held by the ego, or shall we say, the life of self-concern. The reason that you and I have made progress in this work comes from the power of your soul, the entity which selected your embodiment for this journey. So, let us continue with the work."

✳

Meanwhile, in Switzerland, Maia is responding well to her treatments, and Greta sends positive notes back to Crete. One day, when the doctor comes in to do a routine set of tests, Maia mentions that she has missed her period. Another routine test brings the unexpected news that she is pregnant, and after a few questions, the doctor estimates a little over two months. "Does this sound about right?" he asks.

Maia nods, but doesn't respond with visible emotion. The doctor then asks, "Do you want to continue this pregnancy? You don't seem very happy about the news."

Maia says, "I was just surprised, but I shouldn't be. I stopped birth control when I went from France to Athens and the one event was careless, I realize. But yes, I wish very much to keep this child. Will this influence my treatment or recovery in any way?"

The doctor replies, "At this time, the changes taking place in your body can be watched and we can add nourishment to assure a healthy birth. I would say to you, however, that your thoughts and attitudes about this development will greatly influence the outcome of your treatment as well as the health of your child."

That evening, Greta, who is both happy and concerned for Maia, asks, "Are you going to tell your parents?" And a moment later, "And Tonio?"

Maia pauses. "Let me think about this for a few days. My parents, of course. But Tonio I must consider carefully. If my recovery changes, or if I must lose the baby, or if both of us do not survive, Tonio will be devastated, and it were better that he never knew."

"But Maia, you are doing so much better. The prognosis is good after your injections, and if the doctors say that a pregnancy is not a danger, you should tell Tonio. There are rights in such matters."

"But what if his life is taking a different direction now and our lives remain thousands of miles apart, what then? I do not want to obligate Tonio," Maia says.

"How could this be an obligation? He loves you, Maia, I know he does. I see him look at you with such love for you and yet such fear too."

Maia puts her hand on Greta's arm. "I will consider with care Greta. Don't worry."

A week later, after telling her parents and telling them not to inform Tonio for now, Maia composes a long email to Tonio.

Mon Cher Tonio,

Your letter made me sad to know that you are losing interest in your graduate work. I suppose it is natural after all the recent excitement and the wonderful discoveries we have made. Here, I have good days and bad, sometimes feeling sensations of new hope and sometimes some discomfort. But please do not worry about me. Mother says she wishes to write to you, but I forbid it and tell her to let me send her good wishes, which of course I do and Father's, too.

The rains have come to Switzerland and winter is not too far away. In fact, the clouds are only a few hundred feet over the clinic, and I yearn to be in Crete, where it is warmer, and I do miss my family. I am writing this in the main room where patients are playing cards and talking. The wind blows, and it is raining on the window panes. Here, beside the great fire, it is warm. I see your face in the flames.

Love, Maia

Several weeks later, Maia has a general assessment meeting with doctors and the staff. Much to her surprise, they tell her that she is well enough and strong enough to leave the clinic and return home. They give her a complete guide for her next five months, with instructions for diet and exercise and notes for checkups with her doctor in Crete. Greta claps and Maia thanks everyone for their wonderful care. A call to her mother sets in motion travel schedules and a welcome home celebration.

Within days of Maia's return home, a letter arrives from Filiz with the news that site officials from Ephesus have discovered the damaged tholos tomb near the Cave of the Seven Sleepers. Upon examining the remains, they found nothing except some obvious human activity around the opening, which they thought perhaps meant that someone might have been looking for treasure. It was decided to see if they could find the ancient entrance and perhaps fix the damage caused by the earthquake. The discovery of a Mycenaean tholos tomb was a cause for celebration as a tourist attraction. Engineers from Ephesus were dispatched.

The month of November is a traumatic month for the Spiros household. There is concern over Maia's care now turned over to family, an anxiety which is only somewhat abated by the frequent presence of Vassili's physician, Doctor Stavros from Rethymno.

As part of his visits, he asks Maia if she would like to know the sex of her child. When the answer is positively yes, tests confirm that the baby is a girl. Maia immediately names her Sophia, or Sophie as a baby.

Fortunately, Anna's plan to provide evidence of a source for the scrolls in the basement is nearly completed. Workers have torn down a partition between two storage areas and cleared out years of crates and boxes to make a space where a child might play. As they sit and talk about these plans, Anna asks to have the locket Maia has been wearing. Maia takes it off and gives it to her mother, who, holding it, still senses its subtle energy and asks if Maia has as well.

Maia says, "I guess I did at first, but then it just became part of me and as you asked, I never took it off." Anna takes a folded velvet wrap from her apron pocket and gives it to Maia, who, holding it, says, "What is this? Is there something alive inside?"

"We found this in a small alabaster vessel beneath the scrolls in the second amphora. It contained a lock of hair, and I took one strand and put it in the locket. It has served you well, we believe."

"Oh, mon Dieu," Maia breathes, holding the velvet in her palm. "May I see?" Anna nods, and Maia carefully opens the wrap and holds the lock, even smelling it.

"I have imagined," Anna says, "that if these scrolls are Magdalene's work, that she might have wanted to affirm that the scrolls are rightfully from her, even if several were written by another. We will never know, I suppose, but if the single hair in your locket brought healing power to your body, then it is some proof and of course our secret."

Maia begins to wrap the lock again, but Anna says "Wait" and opens the locket and places another hair inside and gives it back to Maia.

Maia says, "Someday I will give this to Sophia to keep her safe. I know that she will have a life of service and great spiritual understanding." She puts the locket back around her neck. "Perhaps you will show me the work in the basement where you say Sophie might have a play space, although her true domain will be the garden."

Anna replies, "And the mountains. There is more to be done, but for the present, the basement rooms are finished. The first task was to install support posts to keep the floor of the Great Room from sagging under the weight of Vassili's library and to temporarily move his desk to the second floor to provide a quieter place for him to work when he isn't in the scriptorium."

Vassili laughs. "Yes, I was exiled for a time from my books, and I feared we might find them all one day in the basement. But as you see, my treasures remain, and Santos, bless him, even dusted them when the work finished."

As Maia settles in and continues her recovery, work on the scrolls progresses and fresh insights emerge every day. One evening, Gregorios comes down to dinner with his notebook. The meal finished, he reads a portion of a scroll that appears to be written by Mary herself.

"My vision of the Master that appeared to me spoke of his love and the trust he always had. He said that he knew that his mind was my mind and that I must share this mind with his followers. He said he did not wish a new religion in his name, but he saw what a new understanding among the Jews must be, a devotion to the Spirit in his name, not of laws and temples but of love and devotion to the Father whose world [or Word?] we have been given. Feed the poor, and clothe the naked, and if the power be in my name cure the sick and care for the children and aged. These are my commands. Love one another and know I am with you always."

In the silence that follows, Vassili finally speaks. "I will let you digest the importance of this piece of text, but I would like to say something about nous, or mind, here. Scholars and theologians will, when they read this, debate the meaning of 'his mind was my mind' from its simple idea of agreement of thought, to the more universal idea of the One Mind. In effect, the battle lines will be drawn between the materialists who believe that matter is the basis of the cosmos versus the idealists who say that consciousness is. We here cannot resolve that issue, but I tell you that the idealists are winning the debate. I am not a physicist, but I can read and what we call the New Physics has broad claims for the belief that universal consciousness must exist in order for the universe to exist, and if so, that I know in my heart that Jesus was telling Mary that both he and she had access to that One Mind. If you wish proof of this belief, just follow the lines of the debate from the distant East to the Hermetica, to Plato and then to Florence and then to Western thinkers who have followed that thread."

"Thank you, Father," Maia says. "Whatever it is that we do with this material must include that principle because, without it, it will be just one more empty theological argument."

Later that evening, when they are alone, Anna speaks to Maia about Tonio. "I must tell you that I have been communicating with Tonio."

"What? Why Mother? I asked you . . ."

"Not about you, dear. I promised as you asked, and it is up to you if you wish to tell him about the baby. Tonio has for several months now been seeing a Coptic priest that your father introduced him to. Tonio is interested in the famous "Discourse of the Eighth and Ninth" and by extension in the presence of the soul. After you left for the clinic, he pressed me about the scrolls, about how I was able to sense their location through Filiz and dreams. At first, I was vague, but he pressed me in such a way that I knew he had not only a right to know but a genuine spiritual interest.

I told him about the dreams and about my own sense of how the dreams are related in some way with the life of the soul. Not knowing what more to tell him, I sent him to Vassili, who began to talk about the Hermetica."

Maia asks, "How long did he stay after I went to the clinic?"

"Not long, less than a month. There wasn't time for Vassili to do much more with the material, but he was able to connect Tonio to the priest near his home, and he has been seeing him and writing to your father and me."

Maia was silent for a time and then, "I don't understand why he is writing to you."

"Ah, well that is the interesting thing. His work with the priest is not what you would call academic. It is functional."

"Meaning?"

"Meaning that he wants to learn to truly know the soul, not just to have some certainty of its presence, but to bring its nature and presence into his life and to his consciousness. Since I said to him that my dreams are related to the soul, he wants not only to understand but also to know, to experience."

"And you think he has made progress?"

"Oh yes, I know he has and that is why I am telling you this. He wrote to say that he had a dream that you were crying out in birth pains, but then you smiled and carrying your child, you walked off into the blinding sun. The priest told him that he had an image from Revelation, and I found the verse. It says, '. . . a woman clothed with the sun, with the moon under her feet, and on her head a crown of twelve stars. She is pregnant and is crying out in birth pains and the agony of giving birth.' I wrote to tell him that sometimes the soul communicates through known texts. A common example is the simple practice of opening a Bible and pointing at a page in answer to a question. Also, as Vassili said, and I agree, the soul residing in Tonio has been embodied in a person of spiritual depth."

"So, you think Tonio has this gift and that he knows that I am pregnant?"

"He wonders. After all, you two have been intimate, so it is not surprising that he would make the connection. When he questioned the priest, he was encouraged to trust the dream. But, because you have told me not to say more than that your recovery was encouraging, I have said nothing else."

"Thank you, Mother."

"Tell me Maia, why do you keep this most important fact from him?"

"I know how some women have sex to trap a man into marriage, and I don't want Tonio to feel trapped. I tell you this because on the night that we made love, it was I who invited him. He was kind and thoughtful and never pressed me. Now he has gone to America and his old life, and I do not wish to leave Crete, especially with Sophia coming. My life is here, and I don't want to force Tonio to leave his life because of me."

"But Maia, he has a right to know that he is a father and you must let him make the choice. I think you may be afraid that he will not wish to marry you and share your life here. Consider carefully."

"We shall wait for a sign, Mother."

GATE NUMBER SEVEN

BETWEEN HIS weekly trips to Allentown, Tonio reads the Discourse of the Eighth and Ninth in the way Vassili instructed. But drifting away one day from the text, he puts the Nag Hammadi aside and writes a note to Vassili:

Dear Vassili:

My time with Father Awasi is going well, and I think we are making progress. I have a question, though, about the discourse: What are the other seven gates? I am assuming that it relates to the soul, but, in human terms, at least, what are they?

Reply:

Tonio. It pleases me that you are continuing to work with the discourse. First, the reference to the Eighth and Ninth refers to levels or gates to the highest levels of spiritual attainment, levels uncommon to human life. To put the matter in human terms, as you ask, the other seven gates refer to our human and spiritual development. Gate one is birth, pure and simple. Gate two is sexuality and all that goes with that identity as we grow. Gate three can be ego, pride, envy, or a natural desire for recognition. Gate four is the domain of emotion and feeling. Gate five is intellect, what we might call self-awareness and the attainment of conscience as a ruling value. Gate six is mystery, a trust in and an elevation in knowledge of your true nature. And finally gate seven is spiritual self-transcendence. It is the level we attain at which the soul is a participant in our conscious life and actions in the world. Of course, there are many levels of development along the way, particularly in relation to what we call ego, that aspect of consciousness that demands attention and seeks to control our life. I think I can say that in your case, Tonio, the achievement of taking responsibility for another life diminishes the strength of the ego and allows progress from gate to gate in the journey of the spirit. You should know that we hear good reports from Greta, and as to the work here, your insights are deeply missed.

With love and respect, Vassili

Tonio is indeed making progress. His time with Father Awasi is, as the priest puts it, "bearing fruit." At home, in his room, Tonio is able to feel each day the energy through his spine as energy in the chakras. High in his back, just below the neck, he sometimes feels something like a vibration, as if someone is touching him with an electric wire, but not so much a shock as a gentle feeling. He likens it to a frisson, that raising of the hairs on the arms or neck that comes from a moment of exhilaration in the theater or concert hall. And he tells Father Awasi that his dreams are more vivid as well. The priest also tells him that he believes that such feelings as Tonio describes are indeed from the soul, the awakened soul to the glory of the creation.

But the real work with Father Awasi focuses on the unity of body, mind, and soul in the serious work of exploration of higher knowledge. The priest tells him that it is not enough to feel a sensation, or to perceive a truth or to acquire faith. In this work, the aim is to be open to perceive unity, a place within where the ego withdraws to reveal a perception of a new reality, one not known before. Entrance to the eighth and ninth gates into that reality will be completely new, something he will come to know and understand, and the frustration may be that others cannot travel there, unless of course they are already in the same space. It will feel like an oasis in the desert, but is a place in the heart, because the realization will take place in the heart as well as the mind as a knowing perception.

At Thanksgiving dinner, with questions coming from his parents about his studies, he tells them that the trips to Allentown have not been very useful in helping his dissertation progress, and that he thinks he will either return to Greece or find another subject.

His father asks, "What does Dr. Burnside think about this?"

"I haven't discussed this with him because I need to make up my own mind about what comes next. I still have my stipend, which is good until June, so I have time to consider. At the present, my heart isn't in it.'

"That's an odd thing to say," his father responds.

"Well there it is," Tonio replies quietly

A week later, Tonio drives to Allentown at the special invitation of Father Awasi, who meets him at the door regaled in his finest garments.

"Welcome Tonio. Today, we will go up to the altar together. It is time to have a ceremony after our time together."

"Tonio says, "I'm not dressed for an occasion."

"For you it does not matter. For me, this is important, and I wish to mark it with a moment you may wish to remember a long after this."

At the altar, where a chair has been placed, Tonio sits, his back straight. Father Awasi says, "This will be our last time together, at least for the work we have been doing, but you are always welcome to come to see us when you wish." Folding his hands, he says a prayer, and then places his first finger on Tonio's head. Tonio immediately feels the frisson, a strong impulse which both surprises and alarms him for a moment.

"It feels like I have bees in my hair," he says.

The priest replies, "You are now outside the eighth gate of the soul, but not yet within. The next step is not in my power but must come as the Spirit governs. What you have accomplished, however, is not common, and you must be careful not to speak of it to just anyone. You will know when you meet another in the same place or realm. Do you understand?"

"Yes, in fact I do. I'm sure I know someone who is in the same place."

The priest nods. "Then you are fortunate because if that is true, you will be able to continue the work. Is this person where you live?"

"No, she is in Greece and is the person who gave me the desire to begin this search."

Tonio and Father Awasi walk to the door and they embrace. "God go with you, my son."

"I feel he will. Thank you, Father."

In the weeks before Christmas, Tonio practices and most times when he sits and puts his attention on his soul, the sensation from Father Awasi's touch comes strongly to the top of his head. At night in his dreams he sees Maia and the others at the house in Crete, and he feels strongly the presence of a baby. But why doesn't Maia tell him? He knows it is his and that the illness must be the reason for her silence. She's being careful, he thinks, not wanting him to be doubly shaken if she doesn't recover or loses the baby. She must be deeply worried now, with another life involved, and she doesn't want him involved also. But would his presence really be a burden?

As if in answer a card arrives from Crete. His mother gives

it to him, with a comment framed as a question. "Here's a card from Greece. Beautiful stamps. A feminine hand?"

"Thanks, Mom," and takes it to his room.

The card pictures a traditional Madonna and child and inserted is a letter.

My Dear Tonio;

I am writing to wish you a Happy Christmas. Here, the day is warm, not too much like winter, although I realize I have not experienced a winter in Crete in a few years. I tested the air this morning to see if I missed Paris. I do not. Mother sends her good wishes and says strangely that she has conversations with you in her dreams.

This rest has been good for me. I have not had to resort to medication in some weeks, which of course is good, given its life-dulling nature. Dr. Stavros watches me carefully. It would seem that I have been given a reprieve, at least for a time. My attention has been drawn in recent days to the scroll work, which gives me a chance to improve my New Testament Greek. Also, we have decided that it is time to make a photographic record of work completed, so I am learning to use a new camera. Remarkable tool because it needs less light, which is good for filming the scrolls.

I photographed a passage yesterday which I found very interesting. Gregorios tells me it may be central to understanding the rest of the work. I have written it out below in Greek. It may prove illuminating for you to work on the translation. Please be patient with it, because it is not clear and there may be missing words and letters. I have tried to indicate lacuna with brackets where they occur.

I understand that this time of year is very beautiful where you are. I hope that your family and friends are all well. Do tell me what you are doing.

My thoughts are with you. Love, Maia

He gets up, goes to his bookcase, and pulls out his Greek/English dictionary. He begins to work on the translation. Maia has written out the Greek in careful script and not as it would have appeared in the scroll. The Greek reads:

Γνωρίζετε ότι η Σοφία είναι παιδί του Κυρίου και ότι ζει με το πνεύμα του πατέρα της που ζει και μέσα μας. [.....] Παίρνω τον πόνο να διδάσκω τη Σοφία στους τρόπους του Πατρός της ότι θα μπορούσε να είναι η γέννηση νέων νόμων και ότι η διδασκαλία θα μπορούσε να εξαπλωθεί στις νέες γενιές ... Ποιος βρίσκει αυτό θα είναι επίσης παιδί της Σοφίας. [. . .]

When he finishes the passage, he makes a clean copy, and his translation reads:

Know that Wisdom (Sophia) is a child of the Lord and that she lives in the spirit of her father who also lives in us. I take pains to teach Wisdom [in] the ways of her Father that it might be the birth of new laws and that the teaching might spread to new generations. Who finds this shall [also?] be a child of Wisdom.

Although Maia could not know this, he knows in a moment that she is telling him about the baby. Tears come as he realizes how subtle her message is and yet how strongly she wants to tell him. He wants desperately to call her or send an email, but he resists. Her message is cautionary, hoping he will understand, but the intended ambiguity leaves him hesitant.

Christmas Day in the Fletcher household, with its eight-foot tree, leg of lamb with green mint jelly, and excess of tastefully wrapped gifts from catalog companies, is, if not joyful, a well-executed family tradition. Out of the silence of eating, his mother says, "You're awfully quiet Tonio. Have you something on your mind? I ask because since that card came, you've been, well, distant."

Then, suddenly, out it comes in a rush. "The fact is that I am in love with a beautiful woman who is at this moment on the island of Crete, ill of cancer, and I'm not there and I want very much to be. And I'm sick about it." He starts to get up from the table.

His mother reaches toward him. "Tonio," she says, quietly "Wait, please."

He stops and sits down again and looks up at the ceiling. "Sorry," he says. "Didn't mean to spoil dinner."

His mother says, "I guess there are things you haven't told us. Do you want to, or is it too personal?"

"This appears to be none of our business, dear," his father says. "Tonio will inform us, perhaps with greater self-control, when he is ready to."

"Right," says Tonio and gets up, slowly. "If you will excuse me, I need to get my life in order." He leaves the table and, taking the stairs three at a time, goes to his room.

Shortly, there is a quiet knock on the door.

"Yes, come in Mother," he says.

His mother enters and sits beside him on the bed. "Why not talk it out? It will help."

Tonio looks out the window for a moment. "I met her in Athens, her name is Maia Spiros. Doctor Maia Spiros. She is amazing, Mother, very, very bright, knows so much and she's very beautiful. I fell in love with her in the Theater of Dionysus the first moment I saw her. And then she showed up with a group of students where I was working, in the Agora. She was their guide and I took them around and later we talked, had dinner. She told me about an important project in Turkey and asked if I could help, would I go with her, and, well, I did, just up and left, which was for me a radical decision. Then we traveled to Crete, and I met her family. You would like her family very much. It's a big family."

"Have you been writing? Is she any better?"

Tonio feels a welling of emotion and a sob breaks loose. He looks down at his hands and takes several deep breaths. "I don't know. I just don't know. We have written some letters, but she's very guarded with me. She doesn't want me to worry, to be there I guess, when things are bad, or get bad. But in the past month or so, there has been improvement, so her mother tells me. I've wanted to call, but I don't want to intrude."

"If you love her, Tonio, and I see that you do, you should be with her, I would think."

"You do? You think so?"

"Yes, I do. If I was loved that much by someone, I would want that person with me, big family or not, no matter what was going on in my life." Her hand smooths the hair on his neck. "You have a good heart, Tonio. You have a great deal to give, but you can't intellectualize too much about things of the heart. Your father, you know, just goes into his study when feelings rise to the surface. Don't retire to your room. I don't think I could stand to have two men I love locked away in their caves."

Tonio puts his arms around his mother, who kisses him. "Your beard scratches," she said, "but I like it. So, what do you want to do? Really."

Tonio says, "To go to Crete for New Year's. To be there."

"Then go."

Tonio steps off the plane in Heraklion just after nine o'clock on New Year's Eve. He tells a taxi driver he wants to go to Rethymno and then sits back to watch the celebration in progress. Kids on mopeds are flying along the roads, swinging party-colored plastic clubs in the air and banging them on the hoods of cars as they pass. The driver, an elderly gentleman with unruly white hair, curses at them and says to Tonio, "This is old tradition in Iraklio. You know the myth of Herakles?" Tonio says that he does. "On New Year's Eve," the driver goes on, "the young ones they drive around and hit people with these clubs. They act stupid like Herakles, the Ox-brained One. They chase the girls, too. Only foolish girls from bad family go out on this night. Nice girls they stay home. These boys wish to be pallicar, brave young bucks. But they are stupid. They know nothing of real bravery. I fought the Turks in Cyprus. I know bravery."

Tonio watches as the shouting boys swing at each other as they pass, going much too fast for the narrow streets. Some have streamers and others plastic string shooting from canisters. Some land on the taxi windshield.

Out of town, however, the road is quiet, nearly free of cars. Tonio feels the knot in his stomach as he contemplates the reality of this moment. He hasn't sent any kind of signal, not even to Anna, who would have told him what was best. It occurs to him that this decision is an act of assertion, a claim to his right to be a part of his child's life. But the Christmas card was a sign from Maia; it had to be. She wants him, not just to be a father but a partner too. What isn't so certain is what this next hour or so will be like. Will the group still be up? Will they be celebrating the new year? Well, he'll see if any lights are on, and if the house is dark, he'll find a room in town and arrive late in the morning, like a sane person.

In less than an hour or so he may know something about what the rest of his life is going to be like. He sits up straight and quiets his mind and heart. In the taxi, however, the effort is difficult. His mind races. That his future depends on Maia is clear to him. The slow ride along the National Road seems now unfamiliar to Tonio. The dark expanse of sea off to his right makes the road seem even more desolate, a road into the void. The driver slumps over the wheel, peering into the night and seems to be ferrying him to Hades. Occasional glimpses of surf breaking are no relief. It looks grey and turbulent, and he's glad he didn't take the over-night boat, even though arriving in the morning might have been more considerate.

Coming into Rethymno, the driver asks where to go. Tonio leans over and points the way up the hill to the monastery. It's nearly ten-thirty when they finally pull through the open gate into the drive. He sees lights on in the Great Room. He pays the driver, wishing him a safe trip back, and pulls his pack from the seat. He waits until the car pulls out of the drive and then approaches the door. He stops, his heart beating too fast, and takes several deep breaths. Please God, let her be all right.

He knocks and waits. It is Santos who comes to the door. "Ah, Tonio."

"Hello, Santos. Happy New Year."

"Thank you, to you also. Please to come in."

Anna appears, beautiful in a long white dress. "You surprise us," Tonio. "We did not know you were coming."

"I apologize. I wanted to call, to ask if I could come, but Maia sent a card with a letter and it said to me that I should be here now."

"Santos, take Tonio's pack. She takes his hand in hers. "Come. We have just finished a late dinner, but we have enough to feed the whole town. Maia has gone upstairs just now. I think she may still be awake."

Tonio looks over at the stairs and Anna says, "Yes, go up."

He bounds up the stairs, turns down the hall and stops before Maia's room. He waits until his heartbeat steadies and then knocks lightly. Nothing. He turns the knob and opens the door slowly. The room is dark, but he can see Maia's figure in the bed, turned on her side away from him.

He steps in and sits on the edge of the bed. At the movement,

Maia turns and opens her eyes. She reaches up and touches his beard. "You are not a dream?"

"No, forgive me, but . . ."

She touches his lips with her fingers and sits up a little. "You did not tell me you were coming. I should be angry with you."

Tonio smiles. "You look wonderful."

She brushes her hair back. "I'm all a mess."

He puts his hand on her stomach. "I know about the baby, Maia."

Maia sits up straighter. "Did my mother . . ."

"No. Maia, I just knew, and your card was like a formal announcement. I will keep it forever. I came because I love you very much, and I want to be with you and see the baby born, and if you will have me, be with you now, always."

Maia sits up. "Are you sure, Tonio?"

Tonio cups her cheeks and touches her forehead with his. "I'm here, aren't I?"

Maia kisses him. "Then I am yours if you will have us."

"I want you both because you are my life and I want our life."

"Then yes." There is a silent moment.

"When does the baby come?" Tonio finally asks.

"In early May. She is due in the first week."

"She? You know?"

"At my age and condition Dr. Stavros wanted tests. A little girl, to be named Sophia, if you agree, or Sophie when she is young. She is Wisdom in the scrolls and for Ephesus and the goddess. She will be a wise child, Tonio." She puts her hand over Tonio's and kisses him again. "Now you must let me get up and we'll go downstairs to celebrate your coming and welcome the new year."

Twenty minutes later, just before midnight, Tonio and Maia appear together in the doorway of the Great Room. Anna stands by the fireplace with Greta and Santos and Vassili, who motors in his chair over to the couple, followed by Gregorios.

Glasses are filled and raised. Anna says, *"Arkhe tou paramyth-iou, kalispera sas."*

Tonio replies "Good evening I got but . . ." He looks at Maia.

She says, "It is the way a myth begins in the Greek tradition. The sense of it is 'Here begins a long story.'"

"Let it be so," Tonio says and raises his glass.

GATE NUMBER
EIGHT

A TRANQUILITY falls over the house, one absent for so many weeks. The basement work is complete, and Vassili is back among his books. Tonio and Maia are discovering one another again through talk and touch, and the work on the scrolls takes on a more leisurely pace, with Vassili and Gregorios doing most of the laborious English transcriptions.

One evening after supper Maia stands and taps her glass, clearing her throat. Silence falls. "Thank you. Tonio and I have an announcement. In order that Sophia be born as one who has all the rights and privileges of proper status in this troubled world, Tonio and I have set a date before her birth to marry . . . that is, with all your blessings."

The company applauds. "What is the date?" Anna asks, leaning over and kissing Maia's hand.

Tonio answers, "We hope that my parents will come, and my father has a time, called spring break, and I checked the college calendar and March 23 looks good."

Vassili says, "It is a lovely time in Crete, not too hot but with many blossoms. We are so happy for you both and to meet your family, Tonio."

Maia continues, "Thank you, Father. We will get our license from the city and we hope that Gregorios will marry us. Gregorios?"

The old monk smiles. "It will not be my first time, but I should ask what kind of service you wish to have?"

Tonio speaks up, "If I may, we would like to have a service we write ourselves. We will work with you Gregorios, of course. We are thinking that our Lady of the Scrolls should have a voice in the ceremony, and that once written down, perhaps Sophia one day will read it, especially since we know she will be a part of the ceremony.

Planning proceeds. Tonio has written to Judith Diels to see if she can attend. She writes back accepting the invitation and says also that she has some ideas about how the work they are doing might be served by engaging the services of specialists in Israel. Tonio mentions this rather veiled suggestion to the group and it is decided to explore Judith's suggestion seriously, but only after Tonio's parents have returned home. Thus, an element of intrigue enters the wedding planning.

One evening, after making love in their new double bed, Tonio says, "I'm hoping that my parents will come to the wedding, but I worry about the scrolls, I mean keeping it all under wraps."

"Of course, they should come," Maia says. "All it will take is a word to the family."

"Yes, I know, but you don't know my father. He will want to know what I'm doing, how I'll support my family."

"Well, that is what a good father should ask his son. What will you say?"

"Probably something very general, but I've been thinking about how the scrolls will make their appearance and what part we might play when they do. The way things happen when historical material first appears, there are conferences of experts reading and discussing finer points and then down the line an official text appears in print to put the new material in the context of the status quo. But what if, as we suspect, the scrolls don't fit into the status quo? What if what they say demands change, is revolutionary in fact? In that case the usual process will demand a whole new approach to the public sphere. After all, we are learning that the scrolls challenge the idea of an organized structure, a new approach to spiritual reality. In fact, what is needed is a remodeling of the whole spiritual enterprise."

"You have been thinking about this, haven't you?"

"Well, my thought comes from something Anna said to me the other day about the Gospel of Thomas, how what Jesus said in that text could have started a revolution, but it was silenced by Church authorities, excluded from inclusion, with no part in Christian liturgy. There is much in that text that could have changed the Church, but it hasn't happened. And we know your father has long agonized over the death of Hypatia and how her story has been lost as a voice for unity and reform."

"What are we finding in our scrolls that could cause changes?"

"Your father thinks that if indeed it is Mary writing, she is saying very carefully that Jesus was wary of a new religion appearing in his name, that it would bring conflict and not greater spirit or perhaps some change in how we understand faith. We're not certain yet that what the scrolls say takes that direction specifically enough. Perhaps your father is reacting to the world we see and two thousand years of religious wars and hatred. But if, just if, what we have is a real means for change, it could support the new forces of spiritual reformation in the world that young people like us are following. Mary could become the inspiration for such change."

Maia buries her head in Tonio's shoulder. "I am sleepy, but I know what you are saying. I wonder if this little out-of-the-way space on the planet can be where change like that can happen. I want so for Sophia to grow up here."

"These days," Tonio says, "there are very few places where

great change can't begin." He kisses Maia's swelling stomach. "Goodnight love, and you too little Sophie."

On the afternoon of March 22, Robert and Ellen Fletcher land in Heraklion and are met by Tonio and Maia. Rather than going straight to the car, they sit for a time in a garden restaurant so that the Fletchers can be properly introduced to Maia. Tonio's father asks Maia about her graduate work at the Sorbonne, a few details of which even Tonio had not known.

She recites the account of an event some thirty years before, when the Greek government hired an American geologist to see where Greece might safely build a nuclear power plant without seismic danger. After almost a year of study, the conclusion was that, no, Greece could not safely build a plant anywhere in its territory. But in the process, the geologist discovered in the fault lines in the cliff face over Delphi a convergence of signs that not only suggested a history of earthquakes, but also provided evidence that two faults converge on the cliffs of Parnassos exactly above the site of the Temple of Apollo. This strongly suggested that there might well have been a crevice beneath the temple, and that in turn suggested that the Italian team that first excavated the site a hundred years earlier may have missed, or even intentionally ignored, the tradition that such a crevice was actually there.

Ellen Fletcher asks, "Why would the Italians have deliberately ignored the evidence?"

Maia says, "The tradition was that the Pythia breathed in emanations from a crevice where she sat on her tripod in order to communicate utterances from the god. Evidently there was disagreement as to whether such a crevice was even there, so the final report said that there was no proof to support the myth. But now, the geological evidence has restored the ancient accounts. And this has meant for this generation a reason to explore the consequences."

Professor Fletcher asks, "Did your work reach any conclusion one way or the other?"

"My work," Maia replies, "took the position that the women who served in the capacity of Pythia for over a thousand years were certainly exposed to some entheogen which was potent, and which produced utterings which the priests formed into mostly ambiguous messages. Evidence also suggests sadly that as time went on there was manipulation of words from the Pythia for political and financial considerations."

Tonio says, "The way of the world."

"Indeed," his father replies.

"What is an entheogen?" Ellen asks.

"Oh yes, I'm sorry," Maia says. "It's a word used to describe any substance, in this case a gas or vapor, that induces an experience which legend calls *en theos*, or to be 'with the god.' In this case, my effort was to return what for a hundred years was called myth to established fact, even with its ambiguity. Whether or not the Pythia were indeed in touch with Apollo was, of course, not a conclusion I could or would make."

"Indeed," says Professor Fletcher again.

On the ride back to Rethymno, with Tonio driving and Maia turned in her seat to answer questions and ask a few of her own, conversation takes a less academic tone so that by the time they enter the gate, Tonio feels that his parents both respect and like his choice of wife and mother of their future grandchild. As his parents get out of the car, Tonio whispers, "Well done."

Wedding day breaks clear and warm. A dozen chairs have been arranged in a semicircle on the patio, where a rented green and white awning offers shade. Maia and Tonio had decided that there would be no procession, so at just before eleven o'clock everyone gathers in small groups. Tonio and his father are talking with Judith Diels, who arrived the day before. Gregorios stands by Vassili's chair, and Greta and Santos arrange a table of refreshments. Maia is talking with Anna and Dr. Stavros.

Then, at eleven, Anna announces, "We are ready to begin, everyone."

Maia and Tonio stand together beside Gregorios, facing the guests. Maia is in a simple white dress, her only addition a crown of white blossoms in her hair. Tonio wears white slacks and a blue tunic with the same flower in its lapel.

After a brief prayer from Gregorios, Maia says, "We are so pleased to be doing this today, with you all here. Tonio and I have written our own service, with the blessing of Brother Gregorios, who has been with our family for many years and is the last of the monks who founded the Brotherhood of the Three Marys here in this house." She glances down to a piece of paper in her hand.

"We have arrived here today, Tonio and I, and Sophia too, who grows within me, at a moment I had never anticipated. Last fall, I was a tour guide in Athens and one day, in the ancient theater beneath the Acropolis, I looked up and saw a man, sitting as if in meditation, at the top of the seating area. As I spoke to a group of students, this man came down to where we were, and we looked at one another for a moment, and I knew in that moment that I would see him again. The love and the vision we now share came more slowly because I was ill and feared I might not live. But the love that has grown from Tonio and my family and no less from the child within me brings us to this hoped-for moment, and we are grateful and confident to say that it now has a bright future."

Tonio, with his own sheet of paper, speaks. "My immediate attraction to Maia did indeed begin in that theater and grew to love when we had our adventures together, a time I could never have anticipated and only now see was meant to be. I come to this moment from the support of my parents and their faith in my choice of career and decision to study in Greece. My fascination with Mycenaean tombs might seem morbid, but I found that their exquisite design shows an affirmation of life and spiritual faith. The love I share with Maia has its relationship with this eternal design, and why I now dedicate my life to what lies ahead, confident that it is an open and affirmative journey before us."

Maia takes Tonio's hand. "My love, before my family and this company I honor you and what you bring to my life and to the life we have before us. I ask for your patience as I learn to be a wife to you and a mother to Sophia."

Tonio responds. "Maia, I come to you with humility and gratitude, knowing that I have much to learn. As a father, I pledge to always ask Sophia what it is she wants to know and do and to support her and keep her safe. And to you I pledge my body, mind, and soul to faithful devotion always."

Maia then says, "We would like to read from Mary Magdalene materials that our dear friend Gregorios gave us for this occasion. 'The Lord said, Blessed are you that do not waver, for where the mind is, there is the treasure. I said to him, Lord, does he who sees the vision see through the soul or through the spirit, and the Lord answered, He does not see through the soul or the spirit, but through the mind which is between the two. Mind is what sees the vision.'"

Gregorios takes both their hands in his and says, "Tonio, do you as husband hold Maia in body, mind, and spirit?"

"I do."

"And Maia, as wife, do you hold Tonio in body, mind, and spirit?"

"I do."

"Then, with God's blessing, I say in the presence of this company that you are husband and wife. You are both precious to me and to Jesus and our Magdalene, who has presided in this place for more than half a century. I also ask for a blessing for Sophia who is to come into the light in your care and may she be a light unto the world. Amen." Tonio and Maia kiss and the company stands and gathers about the couple.

Later, in small groups, the afternoon is filled with talk of what the future is to hold. As Tonio had predicted, his father wants to know where they plan to live and what Tonio is going to do to support his new family. Tonio is as candid as he can be, explaining that since recent repairs were made in the house, various ancient documents and files have come to light, some of which appear to have importance. He and Maia, with help from Gregorios, Anna, and Vassili, will help organize these materials and see what value they might have for the general public—and if they do, how best they might be presented. And as to his graduate work, well, that would have to be put on hold. And so, it becomes clear to the Fletchers that the new family will remain in Crete, but that at some point they will certainly visit America.

Meanwhile, Gregorios, Anna, and Vassili are in the Great Room with Judith Diels examining the library and in conversation about the disposition of the scrolls. Judith suggests that if Gregorios can spare a fragment of scroll material, she has connections in Israel who will date it and formally attest to its age. She assures them that she will not need an entire panel, but only a small piece with a few letters of minor importance, nothing to make news or attract international attention. All are relieved and agree.

The next day, with the Fletchers and Judith preparing to return to Athens on a morning flight, Tonio and Maia are waiting by the taxi with Judith as the Fletchers say their good-byes.

Maia says, "Judith. I just want to say that we are most grateful for your offer to authenticate the scrolls. Do you need any financial support for this work in Israel?"

"Not at all," Judith replies. "Because I'm charged with keeping a record of all ancient sites within the city limits of Athens, I was paid handsomely by the city from its 2004 Olympic funds when they were building the new subway system, when all sorts of artifacts were unearthed. So given my rather frugal character I now have ample resources, and this seems to me to be a perfect occasion to splurge a little. But I have only one request: Please if you can, allow me to take part in whatever comes of this discovery. I can't think of anything more important for my interests and attention in what time remains to me."

As the Fletchers emerge from the house and Tonio goes to take their bags, Maia gives Judith a hug. "Judith, I am so happy to meet you and of course we will include you in our planning. I don't need to tell you to be careful in your communications."

"Not to worry, Maia. I am discretion itself," and she gets into the taxi in the front seat.

After the weekend, the family sits around the dining room table and examines the translations of several letters from the scrolls. A series of iterations have produced what for the moment seems the proper sense both of Mary's words and of whomever may have been writing for her. Anna asks Gregorios to select a passage he feels critical to the discussion.

"I think," Gregorios begins, "Scroll B offers a powerful statement that I believe Mary wanted very much to share, and I believe she did write other letters to the groups of followers that were forming before she died. Anna, would you read the translation?"

Shuffling papers, they find Scroll B and follow along as Anna reads slowly:

I say that to rule is to be confined by rule. To lead is to forget how to follow, and to follow is to understand humility. To demand obedience is to forget how to obey, but to obey is the mark of wisdom. To seek power is to take from the people their own power to know. The power stolen from the people is what takes from the people their understanding. To take power, therefore, is to take away knowledge. To take away knowledge is to take away understanding, and ignorance follows.

Vassili interrupts here: "I must also say here that where we read 'power' in the English can also be 'authority'."

Anna says, "Duly noted." Then she continues to read.

To know God within is also to know God beyond. The Master taught us who we are by teaching us who He is. If the people are treated like ignorant sheep, they will either rebel or they will become ignorant as sheep. If they choose rebellion, they will deny His teaching. And If they choose ignorance, they will never know Him or who they themselves truly are.

Anna pauses and then comments. "This scroll speaks to the dangers of authority and that the more authority or power is in control, the more is lost in knowledge and clear understanding. It should be clear that when Jesus said, 'I am the way, the truth, and the life,' He is saying see my life, how it is, what I do, and if you do as I do, you will find the way and truth and life as well."

Maia adds, "We are aware of what can take place when too much power is vested in people who have authority over institutions, both in matters of money as well as personal behavior."

Gregorios says, "When my brothers and I founded the Brotherhood of the Marys, many reasons came from money and behaviors. We were saddened by the damaged lives of our children who should have been safe in our care."

Anna offers, "Gregorios, you and your brothers were a secret society of the knowing. In the beginning there were secret societies of those who sincerely wanted to know the deepest secrets of reality. As Vassili told us they studied with Hypatia in the Great Library and many went then to Athens and Rome to learn from the followers of Plotinus. And after a thousand years the Hermetic materials arrived in Florence and Ficino translated them into

Latin and the rest, as they say, is history. What we have been given here are words prior to that history and the distortions that such history causes. It is an opportunity to go back and teach as if from a vital present. Think of it as a pure recovery of wisdom, a discovery that might wipe away centuries of error. What the wisdom traditions teach us is that the truth is never to be a secret. It is there for everyone to see and know straight from the source."

Anna's words serve to elevate the discussion to a higher level, a loftier enterprise than what drew them together at first. She asks, "Is this to be another secret society, an esoteric club of exclusive knowers? Or is there another way we can follow the truth to something larger than those who gathered in this house years ago to form a brotherhood of spiritual seekers?"

Maia answers. "Why don't we read some more with these thoughts held close in mind and see how Mary's words might help us proceed?"

Gregorios suggests Fragment G, an account of personal interaction between Mary and the Master.

Anna reads.

At different times in our many talks together, I spoke of my wish for peace, for the fruits of the life of contemplation and knowledge to end human strife and suffering. Finally, one afternoon in the hills between Bethany and Jerusalem, as we looked down from the shade of a spreading tree onto the city in the distance, the Master said these words to me: "Do not hope to see peace come to human life. The Spirit itself breathes in and out; it bends us and breaks us and brings us strife. Only in this tension are we free and able to grow and become divine. What you must seek is rest in labor, a giving and taking always. Seek not repose, which leads to sleep and death." Then, when we sat quietly for a time, He said, "One day, you will travel to the north and you will meet there many wise men, truth-tellers. They will teach you sayings from the East, and these sayings, which are very ancient and have come from my mouth, will speak further of these things. Listen for the truth in what you hear. Many know the truth. Be not narrow or closed to new words and truth that may sound new. The doors of the heart must always remain open."

Vassili raises a shaking arm, "Listen to what Jesus says here. 'These ancient sayings of the East came from my mouth,' another embodiment of the many lives His soul lived before the birth in Bethlehem. Speaking of the north and east, He must mean the Vedic traditions. His soul partook of those words and perhaps even wrote them down first."

"It may be," Maia says, "that we must in whatever form we find to share these words, affirm the idea of reincarnation, which is not only from the East but also from Plotinus and the later Greeks."

Vassili sweeps has arm toward the Great Room. "We have more than one book that describes the memories of people who recall their past lives. It is not strange or sinful to speak of the journeys of the soul. It is time to question how and why the Church took the position it did."

Maia adds, "When I read 'Seek not repose,' I am struck by this admonition not to seek a life of tranquility, but to stay alert and more than that to reach out to the larger world. I realize that when Tonio came to me and then to us that we had been alerted, to know that being here in the security of this island that somehow remains at peace and away from the violence and chaos of the world we are not serving the world, not using what we know, how we know, what it is that must be done." She looks down at the paper. "You see He says prophetically to Mary, 'you will travel to the north and meet there many wise men.'"

Vassili says, "Yes, I have been thinking about that ever since we came across this text. It seems to me that we must let go of what the early Church Fathers taught about the soul, that it is born in us and that when we die it passes on straight to heaven or hell, whatever and wherever that may be. We have an obligation to consider the older tradition of the East, where the soul moves through many incarnations. It is said in the Buddhist texts that the Buddha was able to remember all his previous lives, and we must suppose that his soul passed on to the body of a great teacher, perhaps even to Jesus himself. I think we can conclude from that even now, that the soul in Jesus is with us even now and can teach us still."

Tonio interjects, "Agreed. When Jesus says, 'have come from my mouth,' he doesn't say 'what I said.' There is no me or I there, but rather just 'words from my mouth.' He was the instrument, and we too have become Mary's instruments. Father Awasi said something to me once. 'When the soul awakens,' he said, 'the ego is no longer the master but becomes the willing servant.' We are Mary's servants now and the reason she was hesitant to speak was to find a way to illustrate her humility."

Anna says, "Amen. The Church is full of ego and its soul sleeps."

Gregorios speaks up. "I would like to say something about sin. Vassili and I talk much about the Gnostic Gospel of Mary, which is the text that drew the Brotherhood together in the beginning. And here is the passage that always troubled us: 'The Master said in answer to a question of Peter's about the nature of sin, There is no sin, but it is you who make sin when you do the things that are like the nature of adultery, which is called sin.' And He ends by saying 'He who has a mind to understand, let him understand.' We must take this to mean that we are not born in sin, but either create or engage in sin with our actions. And we do these things in ignorance of the sleeping soul within."

Maia is taking notes and stops and looks at Tonio. "Why do you shake your head?"

"Oh, sorry, but in my spiritual background, the insistence

upon Original Sin was paramount, and I assume also in the entire Judeo-Christian tradition. And I'm thinking, what if that doctrine is fundamentally flawed, what would that mean for the whole spiritual enterprise? I mean why does our Sophie have to be born in sin?"

Anna says, "Well of course, purging Original Sin is essential for any spiritual revision, not only of doctrine but of everything people of faith consider the meaning of their relationship to God. For Christians, the doctrine was not de facto from the beginning. In the gospel of Matthew, John the Baptist announced the coming of the Christ by saying simply 'turn around and see' the Savior who was coming. But in the Greek when John said *metanoia*, the Bible writers chose to say 'Repent' rather than merely 'turn around and see.' The true sense is to change our way of living and seeing."

Vassili adds, "I think, Tonio, that on our part, we left that tradition behind. But what you are saying reminds us where we have been and where we must continue to travel in order to bring about change. It was Saint Augustine in his 'Confessions' who in the fourth century caused Original Sin to become part of Church doctrine, where it did not appear earlier. As a result, the notion that Jesus died for our sins, both mortal and venial, became the basis of Church teaching. It all came, it seems to me, from the problem of explaining why Jesus was put to death. It became a sacrifice, and humanity was to blame."

Tonio suddenly laughs. "Sorry to laugh, but I recall that near my home there was a Baptist church which had a large sign on its lawn that read 'Jesus died for your sins. What have you done for him lately?'"

"Exactly," Vassili says.

Maia smiles and shakes her head. "That is really too sad to be funny." She adds, "What then, does Mary bring to the business of change? Just as Martin Luther raged against the indulgences, we need to rage against the myth of Original Sin and replace it with a positive, a freeing of consciousness, a change so that people approach the divine with confidence and not fear or guilt. Remember, the reason the Church invented Magdalene as a sinner was to make her more approachable for women who felt that the virgin was too pure to listen to sinners."

Anna says, "Well, that brings up the whole matter of prayer, which should also be a theme in our work. Prayer is a quiet waiting for the Spirit and not a series of pleas or confessions. I am always amazed to hear people asking why God allows some terrible accident or disaster to take place, or to assume that because they were sinners, they deserve some terrible thing to happen."

Vassili adds, "Mother Earth is alive, and life is turbulent and sometimes she shakes our foundations."

"There," Anna says. "You see how complicated all this is and what we have undertaken to address."

Gregorios suggests that they turn to Scroll D, Mary's copy of a letter to another woman in Smyrna. Pages turn.

Anna reads:

To my loving sister in Smyrna, who passed such welcome and fruitful days with us here in Ephesus, greetings. You are one who sees as I see and hears as I hear so that we may speak now of a new danger, a new error which those who have no experience have seized upon as the teaching. They choose to believe that the Master died and rose again as an image, to see the great event of our new world, [and] this light that has been given to us they see as a mere painting on the wall, empty of flesh, blood, and soul. Their understanding is a false belief of the senses only, not present in the heart, not present for them in their lives. They join those others we have spoken of who seize [grasp to themselves] the great teaching of the Master as a path to personal power in this world, taking natural power [force] away from those who seem to them less worthy and keeping [holding in] to themselves in order to build empires of obedience. They steal what is not rightfully theirs, what was given to all in equal measure by the Master. This other great error makes my heart heavy and dims the light we faithful ones keep alive. I who saw the empty tomb on that glorious morning, who walked beside the risen Master along the road above the great temple and spoke with Him, I keep in my heart the life and the light of these events. The Master told us that He had come among us to show us a true human being, to make One [unity?] again what had been torn asunder by ignorance and darkness and to teach us that human beings are of the light and that with this light they truly make the world, that the sun, new each day, shines as one on every creature in the world [cosmos]. He swept His hand out [reached out?] into the fullness of the day and told us that here is the Kingdom of the One God if only we have eyes to see. Those who dwell in darkness lack understanding of its true being and their own true being, have fear in their hearts in place of light, have ignorance in their minds in place of truth, and act as though life is no longer theirs. Instead they wallow in their fear and ignorance as abject creatures blind to their true worth, confined to pens and tied to stakes of their own making. In their blindness they pass by the sick and miserable as if they are nothing. They moan and complain of injustice as if they have no power, when all the time they have been given the secret of true human being, true human life. My sister, I urge you to continue to manifest the light with every breath you take. We breathe in the Logos with each breath and breathe out its power again into the world. Do not hide away. Do not keep this light from the world. Finally, in love I tell you this: that the Master bade me come to Ephesus with his mother to drink of the wisdom of the goddess here. May the mind of Him who loved us be with you always.

Your sister in Christ, Mary.

Maia sits up and eyes turn to her. "I have it. When I was in the clinic I thought a good deal about why these scrolls were so carefully hidden. And now that I know they are from Mary and we have here a letter to another woman believer in what must have been a formal gathering, or early church. It tells us that Mary lived a long life and watched the growth of doctrine and the role of new bishops as they established doctrines. She saw the domination of men and the exclusion of women and feared that what she knew Jesus wanted and so hoped would come to pass, she wanted to speak out but could not. These scrolls are her warning both against male domination and imposition of laws. They are proof."

"There is much here to examine," Gregorios says, almost apologetically. "I am moved by the place where the Master says that we human beings make the world and it is our place and that bliss is not in heaven but in the world we make here."

"Amen," Anna says. "The work we have begun is in this letter to Smyrna. If we were to simply read or listen and then do nothing, then we would give away our rightful place in the world we ourselves create. In the meantime, the oceans rise, the air chokes us, and the wells run dry." There is silence.

Greta rises from the table. "Before that happens, I have some greens to wash."

Gregorios laughs. "Good for you my dear, we may survive yet."

Several weeks after the initial meeting to look to the future, a letter arrives from Judith to announce that the Institute of Biblical Archaeology evaluated the fragment of leather from a scroll and determined that it dates to the first or second century CE. Given its rarity the Institute is naturally curious about the source of the fragment, and all that Judith has said is that it came from a monastery in Greece during renovations.

Maia feels the child's increasing movements, what she calls Sophie's eagerness to be born. In the meantime, Dr. Stavros has connected Maia with a midwife, declaring that he sees no reason for Sophie to be born away from home. In the weeks leading up to Sophia's birth, meetings continue and what gradually emerges is agreement that the Magdalene letters should emerge on the Internet. It is Tonio's idea that the site should be called The Magdalene Gates, subtitled, Mary's Way, Truth, and Life.' He explains: "One of the central sources of this work has been 'The Discourse of the Eighth and Ninth,' which is a reference to the stages of spiritual growth to enlightenment." The site will be a place where seekers can enter and be part of a global gathering of those who want to explore their spiritual growth without a set program of lectures, where the Letters will be the core of study and reflection but no organization will impose rules or membership, and no clergy or connection to an existing Church or doctrine could appear or be invited to impose doctrine. The idea of gates is to give those truly interested in spiritual development a visual sense of passing from one stage of growth to another through gates of learning and development here in this plane of existence."

Maia says, "Yes, no one great Pearly Gate guarded by Saint Peter."

Vassili says, "Indeed, it will be a site devoted to both Spiritual Philosophy and Psychology, from both the West and the East. It will be important not to seem as though the people behind the site are all Christians attacking formal religion, but rather are voices leading away from doctrine and separation of East and West."

Anna says, "What I like about this approach is that the offering or work we provide isn't a teaching per se but more of a process, with paths to follow but very personal ones."

"Exactly," Vassili says.

Once that vision is approved by the family, the detail work begins under Tonio's direction. A website has to be built, funding planned, and material assembled and edited. Meanwhile, Maia is in her last weeks of pregnancy, and the household prepares for the new arrival. Tonio and Maia compare notes about giving birth to something new, both having no experience with either.

For Maia, instinct, her mother, and Greta make up for her lack of experience, but Tonio is quite literally on his own and seemingly with no such support. Fortunately, at least he knows what the new site is aiming to achieve and who are more likely to be its followers. And then, to the surprise of everyone and for Tonio's salvation, Santos comes to the rescue. In his room are enough electronics to serve the need, and he is more than happy to sit at his desk while Tonio paces back and forth with ideas and suggestions. Tonio's only comment to Santos when the boy says that he can build the site is, "Were you waiting for a formal invitation?"

Santos replies, "What I said was, I think I can build a site. It requires special software if you want a site built without a template, but I'm sure I can do it."

Tonio says, "Santos, as the new Director of Internet Operations, you find what we need, and we'll build what we need. A program is downloaded that evening, and a new friendship comes to life, much to the delight of Greta and Gregorios.

When the group meets again to explore the content of how the Gates will emerge as a reality, Tonio takes the lead in the discussion. "In America," he begins, "there exists a crisis in the country's religious life. I don't mean its spiritual life because a great deal is happening in that sphere, except it is mostly informal or based on enrollment and/or study. But it is a fact that in the past fifteen years, an average of four thousand churches every year have closed their doors. They just close for good or become homes or community centers. The reasons for failing attendance are many, such as television evangelism, financial strain, and, of course, the Internet. And as hard as it is to get reliable figures, we now think only twenty percent of Christians attend church with any regularity. Life has become so complex and demanding that the idea of setting aside every Sunday morning for church attendance is simply failing, going away. Many are what they call CE Christians, that is, Christmas and Easter. But, and here's my point, it doesn't mean that people are no longer interested in spiritual matters, in whether there's a God or not, or in what happens to us when we die. And, more to the point here, some of the closings must be blamed on outworn doctrines and a rejection of stale sermonizing, not to mention, of course, scandals among the Roman Catholics."

Vassili adds, "In Greece the churches are full of old women dressed in widow's black, holding on to the old ways. And in Europe generally, the decline is worse, I think, than in America. At least America still has the evangelical movement, despite its errors."

Tonio tells a story. "When I was in graduate school, I had a good friend who had graduated from a Protestant seminary and was exploring other options, until one day he announced that he was going to be ordained and perhaps take up ministerial duties. And when I asked him why he made this decision, given his criticism of the Church, he said, "The ark may be smelly, but it's better than the flood." There was laughter at the table. "But seriously," Tonio adds, "now the ark is leaking and quite literally falling apart. So, my question is, How do we address this reality in the imagery of Gates? Do we address what Magdalene reports of her conversations with Jesus? And if we do, how do we avoid not forming another religion, the religion of Mary's Gates to Eternity?"

Anna answers, "To begin with, we show Mary without a church, and instead a woman leading a spiritual life and reaching out as she did to her spiritual sister in Smyrna. It is not possible to address the issue of a failing religion without offending those who are still attached to the need for a structure of some kind. As I see it, we must replace the forms with an emphasis on the role of consciousness, what I call reflective consciousness. If the Gates are to attract attention, I believe we must openly but carefully question those parts of the gospel teaching that describe the foundations of a spiritual reality, one that can be comprehended."

It is agreed, then, that The Magdalene Gates will be a place where people can come to read Mary's letters, download them, pass them around . . . and if they return to the site, they can also explore the latest research into the mysteries of consciousness and also be directed to places, readings, and people who, being of similar mind, will offer commentary based on what they will celebrate as the Magdalene spirit.

Tonio says, "There can be 'Gate Talks' on spiritual development. In an ecological sense it will be a wilderness of opportunity rather than a cultivated space." When Maia asks Tonio what he means by wilderness space, he quotes Thoreau: "'In wildness is the salvation of the planet.' Of course, he meant wilderness, not craziness. In my mind, we're not talking about a so-called 'formal garden of belief' or some such, but rather a natural, undisturbed space where there is an openness where a person can find his or her own path rather than following a marked trail. The reason that we add the subtitle 'Mary's Way, Truth, and Life' is to affirm what is the fundamental core of Jesus' message. The Church doesn't teach those words as existential. Rather they function as though the institution is meant."

Santos asks, "How is a person to choose a path?"

Vassili replies, "A person's Way should be that person's own path. Each person should choose what path to take based on love, and on the Truth that we each are God's sons and daughters, that the soul lives on and is our most precious possession, and that Life is what we make of our being in the world we create. Jesus is a great teacher and Mary His best student, the Apostle to the apostles. I personally love that description of her. She was not just his favorite, but rather the teacher to the teachers. Our task is to purify the teaching as Mary has done for us here. And now that we have her new letters, we have means to share. What we need is a thesis statement, a brief but comprehensive foreword or introduction that states clearly why anyone should be a part of this cosmic creation.

Anna says, "Please Tonio, build on what you both have been saying here. I think we are of one mind. We all should, but only if we are moved to do so, offer words to be assembled into a statement of purpose and shape."

What they thought was going to be a severe challenge turns out to be less so in the light of the scrolls and what was clearly Mary's inspiration. Taking their lead from the subtitle of the Gates, they follow their intuitive sense of where that impulse was received and what it means.

The Way, Truth, and Life of the Magdalene Gates

Welcome to all those who seek to know what is Truth and what is Reality. Is there a God? What is the Universe? What is our purpose? Science, Religion, Philosophy, and the Arts offer some answers. Some accept what parents, schools, and religions teach. Others reach a point where these no longer suffice and they enter cults or take drugs or give up altogether, thinking that Truth and Reality cannot be known or understood.

And yet, it cannot be disputed that the world we experience is full of wisdom and great teachings, and at some point, out of curiosity or anguish or need, we decide to search for Truth and Reality by reaching out to these sources and testing ourselves with and against them.

What we often don't realize is that there is such a thing as readiness, a moment or moments in which we decide to search for Truth and Reality and do so from a position of clarity and freedom. It is fortunate if that is true, and the two qualities we must have then are freedom to explore and a genuine desire to learn. Freedom comes from not being confined to old beliefs or obligatory restraints. Desire means a passion to know and learn, a determination to know, learn, and master.

It is the purpose of The Magdalene Gates to be a place where those with freedom and desire can explore, learn, question, and celebrate the process of passing through gates of knowledge from one platform or stage to the next. The principle is that this journey is individual and intensely personal.

In sum, the challenge for anyone who desires knowledge of spiritual reality is not so much having intelligence but rather an acceptance of complexity and patience with the search. Help, even guidance, is available for those who wish to know and have the desire to undertake the journey. *Welcome.*

When this statement is read to the group, there is general praise and acceptance, with one reservation. Vassili raises the issue of historical education, the notion that if people who come to the Gates wish to participate, there would need to be some explanation of the whole notion of the difference between spirituality and religion and what we mean by complexity. And also, should there be attention to the Wisdom Traditions?

"Isn't it clear what we mean?" Maia asks.

"What I am saying," Vassili begins, "is that when Christianity came to Athens with Paul and was accepted in Rome by Constantine, there were in both places complex and powerful religions already, which we now call paganism. Christianity was formed out of those systems, and what we object to about its forms came in part from pagan ritual, which in Rome were called 'lares.' In fact, we can say without doubt that so-called religion in Rome was not really a new religion at all, but a blend of rituals, most centered in the household. In Greece, too, when Paul came to spread 'the good news,' He spoke of the Logos, a word the Greeks knew from Heraclitus and then adapted."

"That is right," Gregorios interjects. "Look at the Gospel of John: 'In the beginning was the Word,' and in the Greek is *En arche hen ho logos*, and he taught that Jesus was the Logos, the force that speaks the cosmos into being."

"Exactly," Vassili replies. "This was a principle and not a ritual, of which there were many too many. And it means that we cannot wipe away all the symbols of religion, but rather must be clear about the difference between principle and empty doctrine and the errors of authority."

"I would say," Anna adds, "that we must address all the various meanings of the word spirituality as something distinct from religion."

"This is going to be complicated," Santos murmurs, which is greeted by both laughter and agreement.

Greta says, "Santos is right. Perhaps we should start with a website teaching the proper way to harvest olives."

"Yes," Tonio says, "and explain to me the meaning of extra virgin."

"It means cold pressed, dear husband," Maia offers.

With that the serious business of this meeting ends, although what remains is a need to flesh out in the material words like religion, spiritual, and consciousness. But what is indeed fully acknowledged is that real work had indeed begun.

GATE NUMBER NINE

ONE MORNING in the second week of May, Tonio and Santos are in the process of registering TheMagdaleneGates.org when Anna opens the door to report that Maia has gone into labor. Dr. Stavros and the midwife arrive and Tonio follows Anna down the long hall where a bath is being prepared for the birthing process. The midwife has been preparing Maia and Anna for a water birth, explaining that the warm water will reduce anxiety and the buoyancy of the water will reduce pressure and relieve pain, and since the baby is already contained in amniotic fluid, the transition will be less traumatic into water.

Maia is resting in the warm water between increasing contractions with her neck supported by a towel. Anna and the midwife watch for signs of the baby's head while Tonio crouches behind Maia and smooths her hair and massages her shoulders. At the crucial point, with a kind of growl, Maia reaches her hand up and Tonio grabs it and together they push. Sophia is born just after noon on May 8. There is laughter mixed with cheers in the hall outside, partly because just at that moment Santos comes down the hall to say The Magdalene Gates is up and running and he says, "Now what?"

The tranquility that had settled following the wedding returns once again with the birth of Sophia, or Sophie as she is to be called. A small matter like her last name is, for a short time at least, a matter of discussion until settled by Fletcher-Spiros. What no one knew was that in time, Sophie's adult name would emerge as Sophia Gates.

✵

At a very different level of being, the ancient soul that had chosen Maia and Tonio to provide the means for it to come to birth again in Sophia had chosen wisely. From the beginning, this awakened being would make itself known to those who could recognize its presence, and to reveal in that presence its purpose in dream and word and deed and, in doing so, establish an atmosphere and a form for carrying out its age-old vision.

Sophia would be its instrument, sounding the perfect A of the oboe tuning the orchestra of the world to an ancient symphony of knowledge and understanding. Her symphony would suit the time, but it would come from a place so deep that she would hardly conceive of its full nature, even when she knew its source. But only eventually, after the family that nurtured and supported her had passed away, did the soul make itself known to her and give her strength to nurture many souls, whose journeys also possessed knowledge and understanding. She would be an avatar.

For Tonio and Maia, as well as Anna, Vassili, Greta, and Santos, this reality was only sensed as love. Only the old monk Gregorios was able to teach Sophia early on how to truly listen to the soul within her being, to feel the impulses arising above her head as a guide. As a result, the bond between Sophie and Gregorios was strong, and when Sophie began to speak Greek fluently, the bond grew even stronger. The others were surprised as Sophie knew just how Gregorios was able to see in the growing girl how her insight grew and expressed itself, and how her very presence in a group elevated the conversations to higher levels of awareness. There came a day, though, when on a walk with the old monk, Sophie came home alone and told her mother that Gregorios had chosen to stay on the hill where they had climbed, and that his soul had merged with Being.

Sometime later, on a late fall afternoon when the child was seven or eight, Maia and Sophie were sitting on the hillside, near the spot Gregorios had loved, and the air was still.

"It's so quiet, Mother. Nothing is moving."

"Yes, I noticed," Maia replies. "Even the sea looks still."

"I wonder how nature does it," Sophie says.

"Does what?"

"Well, I was reading one of Grandfather's science books, and it said that the Earth travels at 67,000 miles an hour in its orbit around the sun, and the moon goes along too. And the air, the atmosphere, go along as well, and yet here we are in this stillness."

Maia reaches out and takes Sophie's hand and holds it between her palms. "Not only that, the whole galaxy, with all those stars and planets travels even faster out towards infinity."

"Infinity?" Do scientists accept infinity?"

"Many do now. It seems it takes a long time for some people to grow up."

Sophie laughs. "Do you think that someday everyone will know how to understand Spirit?"

"Well now, that's not a scientific question, is it? But I would say that from what I have learned, Spirit must learn to understand just how much people want to understand, and then Spirit might help. It does go both ways."

Sophie takes her hand back and with an elegant gesture waves her arm in the air. "Please, Spirit. Help us understand. You will? Oh, thank you!"

As if in affirmation, the dinner bell rings. Sophie jumps up and grabbing her mother's hand, they run down the path.

All of this, of course, was to be a long time to come as little Sophie took her first glimpses of the light. For this moment, night having fallen of an early June evening, Tonio carries her upstairs to sleep, Maia at their side. The three pause for a moment before the large window at the landing and look out into the darkness. Sophie's breath is warm on his arm. They listen for a moment to the laughter in the Great Room below. Vassili is telling a story. Tonio feels a shiver of an ancient, primal force, and he senses that this child in his arms will, before too many years, walk on a path that he and Maia will not be able to follow, and that her destiny is already being shaped by forces beyond their understanding, out there in the dark, star-filled Mediterranean night.

THE END